YOUTH

YOUTH

Paolo Sorrentino

Translated from the Italian by
N. S. Thompson

MacLehose Press
New York · London

MacLehose Press
An Imprint of Quercus
New York • London

ISBN 978-1-68144-469-7

Library of Congress Control number: 2015951001

Distributed in the United States and Canada by
Hachette Book Group
1290 Avenue of the Americas
New York, NY 10104

Manufactured in the United States

2 4 6 8 10 9 7 5 3 1

www.quercus.com

YOUTH

I

In the clear spring sunshine of a beautiful hotel garden, an unmistakeably British figure sits with his legs crossed; his pale face is flushed red, he has short fair hair, and is wearing a jacket and tie. He is in his fifties, with an intelligent, earnest expression.

Behind him, at a slight distance, are his two younger assistants.

Further behind them lies a superb swimming pool, surrounded by a few bathers, all wrapped in identical soft white dressing gowns, ready for a dip in the sleepy holiday atmosphere of the early morning.

Gleaming hydromassage tubs are dotted about the immaculate lawn.

In the background stands a wonderful Alpine hotel. It looks warm, sedate and luxurious all at the same time.

And framing the hotel are the sovereign peaks of the Alps.

The fifty-year-old takes out a packet of cigarettes and is about to light one when a calm voice, without any hint of reproach, warns him:

"There's no smoking here."

"Not even outside?"

"Nor inside."

The calm voice belongs to another Englishman, in his eighties, sitting opposite. He is wearing a soft jacket and trousers in matching beige and glasses in imposing black frames, behind which nestle pale watery irises, deepened by melancholy and experience. This is Fred Ballinger.

A table separates the two men. Fred has a newspaper open in front of him. He is calm, quiet and self-contained, his eyes constantly betraying a vague disenchantment as he unwraps a sweet that he pops into his mouth with the practised gesture of the habitual consumer.

"Mr Ballinger, may I call you *maestro,* as the Italians do?"

Fred Ballinger gives a shrug. He has no particular feelings about it.

"Are you enjoying your holiday here?"

"Yes, I am. Very much, thank you."

"Have you been coming here long?"

"More than twenty years. I used to come with my wife. Then, as I have so many friends here, I carried on coming on my own."

"But why Switzerland?"

"It's close to Italy. After London and New York, I was the conductor for an orchestra in Venice for twenty-four years."

"Of course, how stupid of me! This must be a very relaxing place."

"Indeed, a most relaxing place. Nothing more."

The fifty-year-old smiles. Fred does not.

"Do you still conduct or compose, *maestro*?"

"No, I've retired."

"Needless to say, like everyone else, I'm a great admirer of yours."

"Thank you."

The fifty-year-old smiles again. "*Maestro*, as I mentioned to you before, I work as the special events organiser for Buckingham Palace."

Fred rouses himself a little. "You work for the Queen?"

"Well, almost, in a sort of a way."

"Good. I find the idea of monarchy touching."

The fifty-year-old is surprised. "And why do you find monarchies touching, if I might ask?"

"Because they're vulnerable. You only have to get rid of one person and, all of a sudden, the whole world is changed. It's the same with marriage."

"Her Majesty would be honoured if you would accept the honour of a knighthood this coming June."

Fred Ballinger lets a small smile escape his lips. "Do you know what Eric Satie said when they offered him the *Légion d'honneur*? He said, 'It's not enough to refuse it, you shouldn't even deserve it!' But I'm not Eric Satie. And please forgive me, I have the bad habit of quoting people. Too much so."

"Her Majesty will be happy to know you've accepted."

"Her Majesty's never been happy."

The Queen's emissary skates over the comment, mildly embarrassed. "Furthermore, the investiture coincides with Prince Philip's birthday and the Queen would like to hold a concert for him by the London Philharmonic at the Wimbledon Theatre to which, for reasons that remain obscure to me, the Prince is very attached, and Her Majesty would be very happ . . . that is, honoured, if you would conduct the orchestra in selections from your own compositions."

"I haven't conducted for a long time."

The fifty-year-old smiles. "I'm sure you haven't forgotten how it's done."

Fred Ballinger gives the matter some serious reflection. "No, I haven't forgotten how it's done."

The emissary gives another radiant smile. "Prince Philip and the Queen will be ecstatic when they hear your celebrated 'Simple Songs'."

With great calm, almost with resignation, Fred says: "I won't be performing any of my 'Simple Songs'."

"Why not?"

"Personal reasons."

"But we can have the great Sumi Jo as soprano."

"Sumi Jo isn't the right person."

"You tell me the right soprano and you shall have her."

"There's no-one who is right."

The decision looks to be irrevocable. Fred Ballinger starts to read the paper again. He has already forgotten all the words of praise. The emissary is taken aback. His head droops.

Silence. The only slight sound is Fred rubbing the plastic sweet wrapper between his fingers at intervals of equal duration. As they alternate, the brief intervals lay down an unmistakable musical rhythm.

The Queen's emissary puts a cigarette in his mouth, raises the lighter to it, then remembers the ban on smoking.

"Forgive me, *maestro*," he stammers out in a last awkward attempt, "but the Queen could take this badly. She isn't used to being rebuffed."

Still seemingly engrossed in the newspaper, Fred Ballinger suddenly stops playing with the sweet wrapper.

"She'll learn to live with it. There are far more important things than my 'Simple Songs'."

The emissary gets up, disconsolate: "Well, I'll report back what we've discussed. Goodbye, *maestro*."

He sets off, his two assistants following. As they move away, they reveal a man at another table behind them who looks as if he has listened to the whole conversation.

He is Jimmy Tree, thirty-four years old, from California, a Hollywood star, and handsome in a dissolute looking way. He is eating steak and chips at this hour of the morning. He looks wasted – several days' growth of beard, dark glasses, his casual clothes all crumpled – and is trying to hide the fact under a baseball hat that does him no favours.

As the three Englishmen circumnavigate the swimming pool to find the way out, one particular figure catches the attention of the royal emissary.

There is a man floating in the pool. Only his swollen face sticks out of the water. He looks South American, his hair dyed an unreal yellow, fleshy lips. He is about fifty, his black eyes are intelligent, his features well worn, but lined with deep furrows that look incongruous in a man still in middle age. He is gazing into empty space.

The emissary stares at him and in a low voice asks one of

his assistants, "Have you seen that man? Is that him?"

The two assistants turn to look at the swimming pool and recognise him immediately. They become excited.

"It certainly is him!"

"My God, it really is!"

The three carry on walking even though they cannot stop glancing back at the South American in the pool who – with the help of a woman of about forty and three pool attendants against whom he is resting all his dead weight – is now getting out of the water and making his way up the easy-access steps. To him, however, they seem insurmountable.

This is because, as we watch him gradually get out of the pool, we realise the man is extraordinarily obese and has immense difficulty walking. Breathless with the effort, this charismatic and cumbersome figure sits on the side of the pool. His arms are tattooed with the faces of famous heroes from equally famous revolutions.

The attendants leave. The forty-something woman with a kindly and patient face seems to be his partner. She sits next to him and starts to rub his hair with a towel, taking loving care of this huge whale of a man.

2

Venice, at night

Every so often, like sporadic irregular implosions from the seabed or deep in the unconscious, the short muffled notes of a guitar can be heard.

What we see now is like a dream.

A very beautiful dream: a deserted Piazza San Marco under the waters of an *acqua alta*. The piazza looks huge, its unforgettable porticos and palaces framing the square lake lapping at its columns.

Across the piazza a long, narrow footbridge has been erected to allow people to cross. But for the moment, no-one is using it.

Then, at night, in this city that is mysterious by definition, Fred Ballinger appears in the distance on the narrow footbridge.

Laborious and frail, he is taking short footsteps, like all elderly people.

Fred looks up. At the other end of the footbridge, he can

make out the statuesque figure of a woman coming towards him. The two continue to walk towards each other, the only human beings in this unreal and flooded Venice. Now they are coming closer, about to pass each other and, with ill-concealed amazement, Fred focusses on the woman: she is one metre and eighty-five centimetres tall, so impossibly beautiful that she seems artificial, with black hair and green eyes. She is wearing a swimsuit with a sash around her that says MISS UNIVERSE.

She is walking along the footbridge with that solemn unnatural strut that top models employ for fashion shows. But the footbridge is only a metre wide, so both move to one side to allow the other to pass without ending up in the water. Inevitably, they brush against each other, Miss Universe's robust cleavage touching Fred Ballinger's meagre pectorals.

He looks at her from the toes up, as if examining something both tragic and benign.

Like all beauty queens, the figure's frosty gaze is lost in empty space and she ignores the ambiguous, fleeting touch of her perfect body against Fred's.

Having overcome the risk of an accident, they continue on their way. Seen from behind, Miss Universe goes off swinging her hips under the full moon, surrounded by the mass of water as if in some dubious dream-like advert for Dolce & Gabbana.

Fred continues along the footbridge and starts to feel frightened – and with good reason – because the water level is suddenly rising. It covers the footbridge, swamping his feet, his ankles, his knees.

Fred tries to move more quickly, but he is old and the water pushes at him. He turns round and gives a strangled cry, as if asking Miss Universe for help.

"Melanie! Melanie!"

But Miss Universe is no longer there. She has vanished into thin air.

Fred struggles a little way forward, the water up to his chest, now his neck, his chin, and in his panic gives another strangled cry when, fortunately . . .

3

He wakes and immediately gathers himself together. He struggles to get up from the armchair. It is late. No-one is around except, far off, a knot of night-owl hotel guests.

Those muffled notes on the guitar are now real and clear and continuous.

Fred sets off, with his usual short footsteps, the underwater lights of the swimming pool providing him with some light.

He walks across the deserted lawn and, over the notes of the guitar, he hears the melody of a song coming from the knot of guests.

The song is "Onward". A wonderful sober example of a modern ballad. Instinctively, Fred draws closer to the music, but keeps to the edge of the knot of people where, guitar held close, Mark Kozelek is playing. There are three women as well as a youth of about twenty and Jimmy Tree. This small relaxed and easy-going gathering is enjoying the Indie American singer's rendition.

Fred Ballinger stops and stands still a little way away and

listens to the beautiful song. Mark Kozelek has noticed him and finds it difficult to hide his emotion at having such an illustrious spectator in his audience. He makes a slight reverential bow with his head during an instrumental break and calls out "*Maestro*" to Fred.

Fred smiles back.

Jimmy Tree, who is lying on the grass with his eyes closed, opens them and sees Fred. They exchange greetings, then Jimmy beckons to Fred to come closer.

Fred obliges and sits on the edge of a sunbed next to Jimmy who offers him a cup. "I secretly poured a little gin and tonic into the herbal tea. Would you like some, Mr Ballinger?"

"No thanks. I would have preferred a little herbal tea in a gin and tonic."

They both smile.

Fred takes out a cotton handkerchief, blows his nose quickly, expertly folds the handkerchief and, with a practised gesture performed countless times, wipes it cleanly across his nose four times, before putting it back in his jacket pocket.

Hidden behind his bold smile, Jimmy Tree has observed Fred's action with the handkerchief. "I was thinking today that you and I have the same problem," he says.

"Let's hear it."

"Having once given in to popular taste, we're stuck with the reputation for the rest of our lives."

"Could be. Popularity's a temptation that's hard to resist."

"I've worked with the greatest European and American directors, but all the public ever remembers me for is 'Mr Q', a dickhead of a metallic robot. On top of that, I had to wear ninety kilos of armour plating. You couldn't even see my face! Every thirty minutes someone reminds me that I played 'Mr Q' and they remind you that you wrote those 'Simple Songs'. They forget that you composed 'The Black Prism', 'The Life of Hadrian' and all the rest."

Fred Ballinger breaks out in a smile and Jimmy too. They have bonded, two subversive partners.

"Pandering to popular taste is a perversion, isn't it?" Fred says. "Anyway, what are you doing in Europe?"

"I start filming in Germany in a month. I'm getting ready for the part."

"Is it a popular character?"

"Depends on your point of view."

"Is it coming along well?"

"We'll have to see."

Mark Kozelek sings the last note of "Onward". The group of friends applauds softly. Fred does not join in. He takes his leave of Jimmy. "It's getting late for me."

"Not for me."

Fred grins. Jimmy raises his fingers to his temple, giving Fred a playful military salute.

Fred heads off with the unsteady gait of the elderly. Jimmy takes a drink and studies Fred as he walks away.

4

Fred Ballinger is standing in the hotel lobby next to the reception desk, waiting for the lift.

A young night porter is staring vacantly at a small television screen with the sound turned down.

A petite, dignified woman, looking older than her sixty years, rings at the hotel door. In a habitual gesture, without taking his eyes off the television, the porter presses a button to let her in. She enters and sits down on a bench staring into empty space, looking resigned.

Fred Ballinger has followed the whole scene without comment. Finally the lift arrives. A traditional cage with a sliding grille for a door. He steps in and goes up.

He reaches his floor and meets a plumpish twenty-year-old girl waiting to go down in the lift. She is not beautiful; pimples stand out here and there on her face, clashing with her scanty attire and aggressive demeanour. We can ascertain that she works as an escort, though atypical for the role.

Fred neglects to glance at her and she pays him no attention.

He sets off on his own with short, slow steps. Outside the room doors, guests' trekking shoes are arranged in a tidy fashion to air.

In the nocturnal silence an elderly man in a motorised wheelchair overtakes him and disappears round a bend in the corridor.

A sound from one of the rooms brings Fred to a halt. Someone is practising the violin. He turns, looking for the source of the sound. The piece starts again from the beginning, two notes played badly, and yes, it is an exercise, one of those tiresome ones.

Fred takes a step in the direction of the sound, but the instrument has been put down.

He is about to set off again when he sees his reflection in a mirror. He examines his face briefly and places a finger on a fresh liver spot spreading across his temple.

5

Those notes on the violin become a soft, distinctly melancholic tune.

We are in a bedroom suite filled with a confusion of papers, notes and laptops lying everywhere, all still switched on.

Four men and a woman, all aged under thirty, are curled up and scattered about on various armchairs and the bed, enjoying the sleep of the just.

Standing in the same room are Fred Ballinger and another elderly gentleman, also in his eighties, still handsome, his hair slightly on the long side, his eyes bright and shining, very much alive and devouring everything he sees. His name is Mick Boyle.

Without breathing a word, our two elderly gentlemen watch the group of young people as they sleep. After a while the sound of the violin fades away.

"Have you managed to piss today?" Fred asks.

"Twice. Four drops. And you?"

"The same. More or less."

"Which? More or less?"

"Alright, less."

"Good-looking, aren't they?" Mick says, pointing at the youngsters.

"Yes, very good-looking."

"You should see how excited they get when they're writing a scene. So full of passion."

"You've infected them."

"Aren't you inspired anymore?"

Fred shrugs.

With his usual gesture, Mick brushes the hair on his forehead with the palm of his hand and then changes the subject. "You see those two?" He points to the girl and one of the boys. The two are sleeping on opposite sides of the room.

"Of course I can see them."

"They're about to fall in love, but they don't know it yet."

No-one notices, but without opening her eyes the girl gives a smile. She is not sleeping.

"And how do you know?"

Mick Boyle thinks for a moment. "I know because I know everything about love."

"Then you'll have to give me a lesson, sooner or later."

"It's a bit late now. Have you heard the latest? Joyce Owens, just crowned Miss Universe, is coming to stay here. As part of the prize she gets a week in this hotel. Gratis."

"Yes, I've heard. Seems more of a punishment than a prize to me."

"And that's exactly how it should be. Some forms of beauty have to be punished so as to make life more bearable for the rest of us."

"How's the script coming along?"

"It'll be my masterpiece. A lasting testimony. And Brenda'll be unforgettable in the leading role. We came up with a title today: 'Last Day in a Life'. What do you think?"

Fred thinks a moment, then says: "It's very good. Right, I'm off to bed."

He leaves the room while Mick goes and shakes one of the young men sleeping at the back of the room.

"O.K., guys, wake up. Time to get back to your own hotel."

6

A beautiful woman of forty is innocently asleep in Fred's bed.

Her name is Lena.

On the bedside table is a framed photograph taken ten years beforehand. It shows Fred with his arms round a woman his own age. They are smiling happily. We can assume she is his wife.

Fred is sitting in an armchair. His eyes are bright with tears as he looks across at the sleeping woman.

Lena wakes. She sees him and looks surprised.

"Aren't you going to sleep, Pa?"

Trying to hide his tears, Fred gives her a sad smile.

"No, I was looking at you."

Lena notices her father's tears.

"But Pa, you're . . ."

He knows what she is going to say. "Don't worry. Old men are always crying for no reason at all."

An early morning frost. The hotel's extensive gardens are lined with beautiful age-old trees. It is dawn.

The plumpish escort and the petite sixty-year-old woman we saw at reception appear. The older woman is probably her mother.

They are walking along, looking disheartened, hand in hand, all but forgotten by the world.

With an awkward and inelegant gesture, the young woman adjusts the very short shorts that have become annoyingly wedged between her buttocks.

Mick Boyle is sitting on a bench going over his work notes. He becomes aware of the women's presence and looks up. Straightaway his eyes take on a melancholic air as he notices that the mother and young girl are walking along hand in hand.

Behind the vast heights of the Alps it is becoming light, just as the frost is melting and dripping off the leaves of the garden's sumptuous plants.

7

A tiny girl of eighteen with delicate features, the very picture of shyness, is giving Fred a massage. He is lying face down on a treatment table.

Lena is by the window of their suite; she notices a man sitting at the edge of the lawn.

"The man who levitates is down there, sitting right below us."

"I've been coming here for years. He's never ever been able to levitate. So, tell me, where've you decided to go in the end?" Fred asks.

"As ever, Julian wants to overdo things. Two weeks in Polynesia."

"Excellent."

"You'll be happy to have the room all to yourself. I was getting under your feet," she says in a friendly way.

"Not at all. You were keeping me company. Mick's working and I'm just bored."

"You won't be bored. I've booked you the full treatment. Massages, saunas, check-ups, doctors, all day long. That way you'll get back in shape."

"It's a waste of time getting back in shape at my age. And all that'll be even more boring for me."

"You do know you're suffering from apathy, don't you? Why don't you go to Venice for the day? You could take Ma some flowers."

Fred makes no reply.

The masseuse is discreet, acting as if she cannot hear.

Lena continues speaking: "By the way, the French keep writing to me every day. They want that book of memoirs from you. What should I do?"

"Let them want it."

She stares at her father's naked body. A body showing all the signs of age. A wave of tenderness crosses her face.

Sadly, she takes her leave. "See you, Pa. I'll call you when I get there."

"Have fun."

Lena takes hold of the luggage trolley and leaves the room.

"Would you mind lying on your back now?" the masseuse asks. She has the voice of a little girl. Making an effort, Fred arranges himself on his back. She starts to work on his arms.

Ballinger closes his eyes, but suddenly he secretly opens one a little, just to observe the young masseuse.

And so the everyday routine of this enormous complex starts to come alive as it provides the services of hotel, health spa, clinic, sports and physical rehabilitation centre, all at the same time, with its set rhythms and well-ordered timetables.

Indeed, on the floors and along the corridors ancient little bells ring out to announce appointments for which one cannot be late.

Nurses and masseuses leave their antiseptic changing rooms in their respective uniforms and set off towards their assignments. Doctors put on their white coats.

And the guests, most of them elderly, all wearing the same hotel-issue dressing gowns, form orderly queues for the various check-ups, swimming pools, saunas and massage rooms.

The silent, small and peaceful comings and goings of a world getting started.

In the dim light of the breakfast room, the waiters are setting the tables again. An anorexic chef makes it to the back of the kitchens and enjoys the first drag of a cigarette while he looks up beyond the Swiss mountains at the sky's luminous blue.

8

Soporific New Age music pervades the massage room.

The subdued lighting is augmented by a sea of candles placed all around.

Fred is stretched out comfortably in an enormous cradle of straw as if he were an eighty-year-old Baby Jesus in his crib.

A small Thai man of about fifty is scattering burning-hot black stones over his body. Each time a stone is placed on him, Fred lets out a slight cry of pain.

The masseur laughs. In hesitant English he says: "After pain comes pleasure."

"Before the pain starts again," Fred concludes.

9

Later on a nurse takes a blood sample from Fred.

A doctor in his sixties enters the room. He has a likeable and good-natured face.

"How are we getting along today, Mr Ballinger?"

"Well, we're getting along. I'm not sure where to, but we're getting there."

The doctor smiles, then stops to examine Fred's face. He slips on his spectacles and looks even more closely.

"My daughter says I suffer from apathy. Does it show much?"

The doctor smiles again. "Would you like to have these age spots lasered?"

"No, I wouldn't. Why?"

"Because they're not aesthetically pleasing."

"But they remind me of something fundamental."

"What's that?"

"That life is full of blemishes."

The doctor and Fred smile at each other. The nurse has finished taking the sample.

Fred looks out of the window that frames an unblemished Alpine peak outlined against a blue of singular clarity. His expression is now serious.

IO

The young scriptwriters are in the middle of a slanging match. Submerged by the sea of papers in his suite, Mick listens to them without intervening. Fred enters the room, but no-one pays him any attention. They are all too busy arguing. He listens to them in a disinterested way.

Everyone is talking over everyone else, but two voices manage to shout more loudly and attack each other more savagely.

Of course, these two are the young man and woman that Mick maintains are on the road to reciprocal love.

"You've just seen too many movies, you idiot, and forgotten about real life," he screams.

"Movies *are* life! All you do is criticise! You've never once had any inspiration," she shouts back.

He laughs and applauds sarcastically.

A shy scriptwriter, sitting near Mick, comments on the row in a low voice: "Exactly!"

"Inspiration? Didn't they tell you at film school that inspiration doesn't exist? It's a myth. There's no such thing as inspiration, only the fermentation of ideas."

"Exactly!" the shy scriptwriter confirms.

"Oh, but inspiration does exist, it does," the girl insists. "But as you haven't an ounce of talent you can't recognise it."

"Exactly!" the shy scriptwriter adds again.

Mick notices his neighbour's shifting allegiances and turns on him sharply: "What the hell? Are you just agreeing with everyone?"

"Of course! I'm insecure and fearful. My parents never encouraged me. My brother's favourite sport was using me as a punchbag. My sister called me 'Loser'. I've never had a girlfriend and I have a huge hang-up about my sexual identity."

This has Mick laughing.

"Stop it! You'll never get me to feel any sympathy."

"I have an aunt who had polio."

Mick laughs again.

"I won't allow you to say I don't have any talent any more, you idiot!" the first scriptwriter replies, brimming with anger.

"Isn't it time you got on with your fermentation then, you talentless parasite?"

"That's enough! I'm shocked at you," Mick says, interrupting them. "We have to come up with an ending and you're wasting time by talking about the wider scene."

Fred offers a suggestion: "But they're right. Individual scenes all hang on the wider one."

Only now do they notice him.

"Ah, it's you, Fred. Listen, I need to be here for another couple of hours, then I have to talk to the doctor. I'll catch up with you after that, O.K.?"

"Alright."

Gloomily, a little disappointed that no-one has responded to his remark, Fred leaves the room while Mick spurs on his scriptwriters.

"Well, what about it? We need an idea for the ending."

One of the boys, who so far has made no contribution, butts in. He has a long beard and messy hair, the very image of the cultivated and ironic intellectual. As if coming out of a vision, he says dreamily: "As he's about to die, the man whispers feebly to his wife: 'Don't cry, my dear. You know I've always found women who cry shallow and repellent.'"

The two who were arguing look at each other and burst out laughing.

The shy and insecure scriptwriter reflects a moment and pronounces with some assurance, "Great idea!"

Mick shoots him a look of disgust, then comments: "No, that's a crap idea. Anything else?"

II

The hotel guests are in a torpid state, as if under anaesthetic. Addled by the silence, they observe a swarm of wealthy Russians dropping themselves slowly onto the sunbeds first thing in the morning and then the stillness of an attractive African-American family floating in the swimming pool.

In one corner, in the shade of a canopy, you can enjoy a massage in the open air. Two young adolescents are hanging around there, overcome by a flood of hormones, stealing sidelong glances at a beautiful woman having a massage.

Few guests, but all wealthy.

In the sky against the clear outline of the Alps, it is possible to make out the distant shapes of two paragliders. A pair of elderly gentlemen have dozed off in their motorised wheelchairs. Their Asian carers are as discreet and quiet as mice.

A man in his fifties is doing gymnastics along with his decrepit father.

At the bottom of the garden, separated from the rest by a hedge, the obese South American, resting on his stick, is signing autographs for a mixed group of people, all of them enchanted by the sight of this sporting legend. At his side, his companion – ever worried about her man – keeps time on the signing. Someone takes a photo on their smartphone. She explodes and stops anyone else who dares to take a photograph.

From a sunbed, dressed in a white dressing gown, Fred Ballinger sucks on a sweet and watches with resigned interest as the autographs are ritually doled out by the South American. With the one hand that dangles free from the sunbed, he smoothes the sweet paper at irregular intervals, giving life to an accomplished rhythm.

Jimmy Tree is on the sunbed beside him and he too is closely observing the South American, but Jimmy's attention is focused principally on the man's briarwood walking stick with its twisted nodular shape and antique finish.

Jimmy then looks around and something else catches his eye: a mother spreading suntan lotion on her thirteen-year-old daughter.

This young girl, whose skin is so white it is almost transparent, stares at the ground as if about to faint from pathological shyness. Then, for no apparent reason – she must have become nervous – she starts gnawing at her fingernails with extraordinary voracity. Then the mother must have told her to stop, because the girl screams at her, gets up and hurries away.

With an unlit cigarette dangling from his lips, Jimmy cannot help but watch this scene in the same way an entomologist studies insects.

Supported by the stick and his wife, the South American is

coming back up the garden. They walk past an empty tennis court, and the man's attention is caught by a forgotten tennis ball lying on the ground.

Fred and Mick are next to each other at the chemist's counter.

Fred waits while Mick, his glasses perched on the end of his nose, carries out a thorough check to see if the chemist is doing everything correctly.

In fact the man in the white coat is organising the numerous boxes of medicine in front of Mick into a sizeable mountain of pharmaceuticals

"That's everything."

"Good." Mick turns to Fred and only now realises his friend has bought nothing for himself. Puzzled, he asks him, "Don't you have to take anything?"

So Fred, feigning uncertainty, looks about him and his eyes fall randomly on the first shelf in front of him. It holds various types of plaster.

Fred takes the first box that meets his eye and places it in front of the chemist.

Mick has followed his every move.

"What do you need plasters for?"

"Nothing. I'm getting them to show a little solidarity with you."

His friend turns and looks at his mountain of medicines and says, half seriously and half in jest, through clenched teeth, "Oh, go fuck yourself, will you?"

Fred Ballinger's face breaks out in a sardonic smile.

12

Fred and Mick are walking in a scenic valley, through a meadow. To the right it gives way to a stretch of woodland, and to the left it flanks a village in Alto Adige, across the border in Italy.

They are chatting away.

"Why do you think we keep coming here, year after year?" Fred asks.

"Because we like coming back to the places that have made us happy."

Fred chuckles. "This is the scriptwriter talking."

"If only! It's John Cheever."

"Do you remember Gilda?"

"You mean 'Gilda' the film?"

"No, Gilda Black. That girl we both fell in love with."

"Gilda Black?"

"Gilda Black."

Mick laughs. "The things you bring up! That must have been a hundred years ago."

"To me it seems like yesterday. I'd have given twenty years

of my life to have gone to bed with her."

"Then you'd have been a fool. Gilda Black wasn't worth twenty years of anyone's life. Not even a single day."

Fred is suddenly extremely disappointed and also a little uneasy. "And how would you know? Did you go to bed with her?"

Mick starts to stammer, knowing he has put his foot in it. "What's that? What did you say?"

"You heard me very well. Sixty years ago you swore you hadn't gone to bed with her out of respect for my love for her. Now you're telling me something different."

"Look, there's something I have to confess to you."

"Oh, bravo, let's hear it!"

"The real tragedy – and believe me, it really is a tragedy – is that I can't remember if I went to bed with Gilda Black or not."

"Are you serious?"

"Unfortunately, yes. I swear."

"O.K., well, that changes everything."

"In what sense?"

"If you had been certain you'd gone to bed with her, our friendship would be over. But now, well, let's say . . . I can live with the doubt."

"And anyway, if I did go to bed with her and I can't remember now it means she wasn't worth your twenty years of life. Don't you think?"

"Yes, you're right. So between the two of us, we can draw a line under Gilda Black?"

"Good. Have the kids left?"

"Your son likes to do things in style. Polynesia."

"I know. He spends money like water, that one. I wonder who he got it from."

"Not from you, that's for sure."

Mick laughs. Silence. All of a sudden, Fred loses his patience. He sighs.

Mick notices. "What's up? You're not still thinking about Gilda Black, are you?"

"No, I'm thinking about the things that, as time passes, we can no longer remember. I can't remember my parents anymore – how they looked, how they spoke. Last night I was looking at Lena as she was sleeping and I was thinking about all those little things, thousands of things, I did for her as a father. And I did them for her with the precise intention that, when she was grown up, she'd remember them. But as time passes, she won't remember a thing."

Mick looks at him and cannot say a word. Then Fred stares up at Mick and with a slight, though uncharacteristic, show of emotion, he takes his arm and whispers angrily: "Huge efforts, Mick. Huge efforts that come to nothing. It's always the same."

Mick is surprised and looks blank. "This discussion's becoming interesting. I need a cigarette, but I left mine in the hotel. Wait for me here while I go and buy some."

Fred nods sadly, as if defeated.

His friend goes off to the village.

Out of the silence, the intense chirr of a cicada strikes up. Fred turns towards the source of the sound, drawn towards it as if in a dream.

*

He ends up among the trees, where there are hundreds of cicadas. Then a bird starts up a strange mean-spirited twitter, drowning them out. Fred is attracted by this new sound. He forgets about the cicadas and goes off to find the bird. He stares up into the trees, looking for it, but the bird keeps itself hidden. Fred walks on towards the edge of the wood. A newcollection of sounds is added to the chorus. Cowbells.

Fred comes out of the woods and an immense soft hillside opens before his eyes in the sunlight. Dotted about the meadows are fifty or so grazing cows shaking their fifty or so bells at random. His eyes light up at the scene. He sits down on a rock, still staring at the cows.

He listens to the discordant layers of sound: cowbells, cicadas, bird.

At this point, Fred concentrates and closes his eyes. Very gently he starts to move one hand just like a conductor and, as if he had conjured a spell, several of the cowbells fall silent. Others are still ringing; they no longer create an anarchy of sound, but rather the notes are rolled out in a melodic manner. With another wave of his hand, Fred elegantly stops the remaining cowbells so that only two are left ringing out in alternate notes.

A grand gesture of his arm, as if directed behind him, and the bird in the wood joins in with the two cowbells. Then, with both his arms, Fred invites the chorus to join in: hundreds of cicadas accompany the bird's solo and the counter-melody of the cowbells to create a symphony of nature.

Fred still has his eyes closed and is smiling to himself. For the first time he appears to be happy.

Selecting the sounds he has to play with, he is engaged in something wonderful. He is composing.

Mick comes back to the spot where they left each other in the meadow. He looks around, but there is no sign of Fred. He lights a cigarette. While doing so, his eyes make out something moving in a distant paddock. A white horse.

Mick then does the only thing he knows how to do: he places the fingers of both hands together, as film directors do, to simulate the frame of a camera image. He closes one eye and, making a tracking shot with the rectangle formed from his fingers, he follows the beautiful horse as it trots around.

13

A footbridge behind the hotel connects the building to the mountainside. A dozen or so waiters, chefs and nurses are spread along it enjoying a moment of free time.

All are having a smoke, chatting away and joking as they take a break.

One figure stands away from the rest. She is smoking, but speaks to no-one. She seems very depressed. Leaning over the railing, she stares down at the ground without any interest. It is the masseuse who came to Fred's room.

Fred is in one of the hotel corridors looking out through a window. His face is also filled with bleakness as he watches the lonely girl smoking and looking down over the railing.

The sound of the violin playing the same exercise attracts Fred's attention. He goes off in search of it.

14

Fred moves cautiously along the empty corridor. The violin can be heard more clearly. He meets the sixty-year-old doctor with the friendly face followed by two nurses. He exchanges greetings with the doctor.

He comes to a room with an open door. The chambermaid is finishing tidying up and behind her, close to a mirror, standing in front of a sheet of music, a boy of twelve is practising endlessly those same two notes.

The chambermaid leaves the room with her trolley.

Instinctively Fred draws near to the threshold and watches the boy as he practises. The boy senses his presence and turns to look at him.

Fred gives him a smile. The boy returns it.

"Do you know who composed that piece you're practising?" Ballinger asks, a hint of emotion in his voice.

"No. Who?"

"Me."

"I don't believe you. What's the piece called?"

"It's called 'Simple Song, Number 3'."

The boy checks the sheet music. "That's right. And what's the composer's name?"

"Fred Ballinger."

"And what's your name?"

"Fred Ballinger. You can check down at reception. I'm a guest here in the hotel."

The boy now shows some surprise. "Unbelievable."

"Yes, unbelievable."

"My teacher makes me play it because he says it's an excellent piece for a beginner."

"Yes, he's right, because it's a simple piece."

"But it's not just simple."

"Oh, no?"

"It's also a very beautiful piece."

Despite his composure, Fred instinctively allows himself to say something warm and friendly.

"Yes, it's very beautiful. I wrote it when I was still capable of love."

The boy seems not to have understood the last remark very well and, as if nothing has been said, starts practising again.

Fred listens to him and then interrupts the boy again. "May I do something while you're playing?"

Slightly unsure, the boy nods. "Alright."

He starts playing again.

Fred cautiously enters the room and goes up to the boy.

The boy carries on playing. Fred raises his hand and moves the boy's elbow three centimetres in order to correct the position of the bow.

He then closes the door behind him with a sense of accomplishment.

"That's it. Much better."

15

Only the clashing of cutlery breaks the lugubrious silence of wealthy people eating.

The Russians, the African-American family and the hordes of elderly are having dinner in the hotel. But most eyes are irresistibly drawn to the famous obese South American who is sitting with his wife, eating in silence.

On one table, a youth of twenty finds it difficult to resist temptation and surreptitiously lifts his iPhone to take a shot. But the sporting legend has noticed. He confines himself to a tired gesture to his wife who immediately understands. She gets up and fetches a screen standing by a column. She places it between her husband and the rest of the dining room, then disappears behind it.

Jimmy Tree is eating on his own and has been watching the scene play out with concentrated intensity.

Among the bystanders there is also a man of fifty, a colossus with a very thick beard, dishevelled hair and wearing the remnants of an Alpine mountaineer's outfit. He looks like some latter-day hippy. He is tackling a bowl of broth with a linen napkin tucked into his shirt.

The overweight South American has finished eating and is now crossing the room with his stick, supported by his companion, clearly proving how great an effort it is. As he passes, everyone sneaks glances at him. But Jimmy Tree's attention is once again focused on the man's walking stick.

At another table sit Fred and Mick. They are obsessed with watching a very distinguished couple in their sixties, never taking their eyes off them. From their features you would say they were German. They are both dressed in matching brown and beige and not simply by coincidence. They both look extremely bored, lost in space, and never exchange a word.

Fred and Mick continue chatting, but never take their eyes off the silent couple.

"Where did you get to today?" Mick asks.

"I got lost following the sounds of nature."

"But isn't it music that you lose yourself in?"

"'Any sound can become music,' as Stockhausen said. And what did you do?"

"I couldn't find you, so I went and had a chat with my medical friend. They'll speak tonight, you just see."

But the German couple across the room are silent.

"Thirty francs they don't say a word throughout the whole meal," Fred says.

"I'm sure they'll speak. Let's make it fifty."

"Done."

The couple gets up, the man very courteously drawing back his wife's chair. She takes his arm and they depart. Fred and Mick watch them right up to the door. The couple have not said a word.

"That's 250 francs you've lost this week." Fred blows his nose, wipes the handkerchief four times across it, then folds it and puts it back in his pocket.

Mick Boyle brushes the palm of his hand over his hair.

From his table Jimmy Tree has been watching their every movement.

16

A swing orchestra is performing on a stage in the garden. It tries to liven up the evening with a piece that is supposed to be full of joy, but only ends up generating a vague sense of congeniality.

Four old men sitting in motorised wheelchairs around a table make up a game of ten-card *scopone*.

Only a few people are willing to dance and do so awkwardly.

A Russian man and his wife spin around, sweating as if taking part in a contest. He has her perform the *casqué* of the tango. She laughs.

Looking incongruous in his sunglasses, Jimmy Tree is in a corner chatting to his friends, among whom is the musician Mark Kozelek.

"What time did you come down for dinner?" Mark asks.

"Very early," Jimmy replies.

"If you'd called me I'd have come down with you."

"That's O.K., I wasn't only having dinner."

"What else were you doing?"

"I was working."

At their table Fred and Mick are lazily observing the dismal evening.

The song ends and the orchestra begins a slow number. More couples get up.

The eternally silent Germans also move onto the dance floor. They dance with conviction, but exchange neither a word nor a glance. The woman stares expressionlessly at Jimmy Tree. He notices and lowers his sunglasses to give her a friendly smile. She does not smile back, nor make any other gesture, but her husband has followed everything, feeling both serious and jealous.

Wistful and alone, the hippy mountaineer watches the swing band while he sips a hot tisane that scorches his lips, so that he gasps with each mouthful.

Mick and Fred allow themselves a rapid exchange on a painful subject.

"Anything today?"

"Nothing at all. You?"

"Nothing either."

"Well, let's hope for a piss tomorrow."

Making a tremendous effort, the South American with the stick gets himself to the middle of the dance floor. He smiles and holds out a hand, inviting his companion to dance. With a radiant look, she runs over to him. They dance for ten seconds, during which time the man struggles against his obesity, his knees crumbling under the weight. He then stops, exhausted. His companion looks concerned. She makes a sign and two diligent waiters carry a chair onto the middle of the dance floor. The man collapses into it and seems to be able to breathe again.

Everyone follows these proceedings with concern.

Fred and Mick are no exception. Fred blows his nose in his usual ritual way.

"That man's the last true legend on Earth," Mick says. "Just like in Ancient Greece. Anyone else in his place would have made people laugh with such a performance. But no-one laughed. You know why?"

"No, why?"

"Because a legend makes no provision for the ridiculous."

17

Fred is walking along a hotel corridor. He is retiring to his room. He is overtaken by an elderly man on a mobility scooter. The man comes to an L-shaped bend that turns into another corridor and he runs into another mobility scooter that pops out from the right. This gives rise to a minor but very real traffic accident and to an altercation between the two men about rights of way and careless driving.

Fred watches the scene without batting an eyelid while he inserts his key into the lock and disappears into his room.

18

Fred is in his room. He starts to undress. As he is taking off his shirt, his attention is caught by an inexplicable muffled sound coming from the bathroom. He goes over to open the door and finds his daughter Lena sitting on the edge of the bath, sobbing, wallowing in tears. Fred is taken aback and, for a moment, speechless. "What are you doing here?"

Still in tears, she makes no reply.

"Shouldn't you be on a plane to Polynesia?"

She sobs even more loudly.

"Where's Julian?"

Lena emits a word that comes out like the moan of some strange animal. It is difficult to understand what she says. She goes back to her tears.

"Well, are you going to answer me?"

But she says nothing. She cannot say anything. She can only cry.

19

Mick Boyle is lying fully dressed on the bed surrounded by papers and laptops, chatting away happily on the telephone despite it being the middle of the night.

Pacing about the room, concentrating hard and anxious to know the outcome of the call, are his young scriptwriters.

"Very good, Nick. I'm glad you find the second draft convincing . . . Yes, we're still working on the ending, we're not entirely satisfied with it either . . . I've spoken to Brenda. Everything's fine . . . Yes, of course she can't wait. I mean, how often does she come across a character like that at her age? Yes, I know, she's fickle, but she's fine with me. She's always saying I'm the best in the world with actresses, that I'm the only one who knows how to deal with them. I'll start searching for locations next month, if you're agreeable . . . Perfect. Great. *Ciao.*"

Happy with the result, the scriptwriters exchange smiles and pats on the back.

Mick replaces the receiver and looks up.

Only now do we discover the presence of Fred Ballinger sitting in an armchair.

"What's the matter with you? You're pulling such a long face," Mick asks him.

"Your son has just left my daughter."

"Shit!" a scriptwriter says.

"You what?"

"They were just boarding the plane and on the gangway he stopped and told her he had fallen in love with another woman."

"Yes, gangways make you feel as if you're on a gangway, on the edge."

"How very profound! You're a real wizard with the metaphor, aren't you?" Fred replies, full of irony.

The scriptwriters snigger.

"And so he's gone off with this other woman?"

"No, it appears he's had the decency not to do so. At least up till today."

"And Lena?"

"Lena's in my room. She can't stop crying. I've never seen a person cry so much in all my life. I didn't think you *could* cry as much as that."

"One time," Mick says, "I read in a magazine that the tear glands can produce enough tears for three whole days without stopping."

"I knew that. I saw it in a B.B.C. documentary," the shy scriptwriter adds.

"On the point of death our protagonist says to his wife, 'My love, let's watch a last B.B.C. documentary together,'" the team's resident intellectual throws in.

Fred is upset. "That's enough, kids."

"I'm not sure it's true about this business of the tear glands, you know. It was in one of those popular magazines that tend to hype things up to sell a few more copies."

"I think we're getting away from the subject here."

"You're right. What a dickhead Julian is. Just like his mother. You remember? I worshipped her, while all she worshipped was stagehands and electricians."

"She would worship anybody, Mick."

The one female scriptwriter smiles. "Ecumenicalism is a noble ideal."

"Ecumenicalism?!" Mick says, feigning anger. "My best friend is saying that my ex-wife would go to bed with anyone and in all these years he's never said a word to me. Don't you realise how serious this is?"

"Like you never told me about Gilda Black."

"Alright, I get it, you want revenge. And now you've had it. But let's get real here. I want to hear what that dickhead of a son of mine has to say."

Mick grabs the telephone again and dials.

"What are you doing? If you're thinking you can persuade him to go back to Lena, it's pointless."

"No, but at least I want to understand."

His son must have answered because Mick starts to speak in an angry voice. "I'm your father, but on the basis of recent evidence I'm not so sure that you're my son."

The intellectual scriptwriter nudges the shy one: "Make a note. We'll put that in the movie."

20

It is late for breakfast. Some waiters are already laying the tables for lunch. There are no other guests, apart from the eternally silent couple who finish, leave the table and go out as usual without having said a word.

Mick and Fred watch them leave and when they disappear a disconsolate Mick mechanically takes out fifty francs and hands them over to Fred.

"How do you always know with such certainty that they won't say a word?"

"Because a waiter told me something about them."

"What was that?"

"I can't tell you. It's the edge I have over you."

"You just tell me right now! Anyway, that waiter'll tell me. I'll bribe him. At this point, with all the money I've blown on it . . ."

"Oh, alright, I'll tell you. They're deaf."

"You dickhead! You can just give me back all the money I've shelled out, right now. You're a crook. The bets are all null and void."

"You know, you really are naïve! I was only joking. They're not deaf at all."

The conversation is interrupted by a silent apparition at the other end of the room: a forty-year-old man in immaculate jacket and tie, followed by a woman, also in her forties, who appears to be his secretary, frumpy and non-descript, hair done up as best she can, wearing no make-up, but respectably dressed in cheap clothes.

Mick and Fred look sternly at the man coming towards them. While he walks up to them he hands his smartphone to the secretary who slips it into a leather briefcase.

The man in the jacket and tie comes to a halt in front of Mick and Fred's table. The woman stays a few metres behind and fiddles around with some e-mails on the smartphone.

Mick looks at him. It is by now clear that this is his son, Julian. He is an incredibly handsome man, objectively so, immaculate. Confident and sure of himself, he returns his father's gaze. Fred's eyes dart from one to the other as if watching a tennis match.

"What the bloody hell is all this business?" Mick asks.

"It's a very simple business, Dad. I've fallen in love with another woman."

"And I bet she's eighteen, right?"

"She's not eighteen. She's thirty. A perfectly reasonable age."

"Whatever age she is, you've screwed up."

"That's your opinion."

"Yes, it is my opinion. Lena's a woman of exceptional merit. Of course, I realise at this point she's wasted on you. Too intelligent for you."

"She probably is. Why have you made me come here? I'm not going back on what I've done."

"That's what they all say to start with. Then they beg the wife or husband to take them back. Do you know how many I've seen . . ."

"Mother left you and she never begged to get back together with you."

Mick turns to Fred. "What was I telling you? Can you see who this little shit takes after?"

"Tell me, is a man a little shit just because suddenly, against his will, and having struggled like a madman to stay with his wife and booked a dream holiday with her, he simply doesn't go because he's fallen in love with another woman?"

"Just like your mother! Melodramatic, rhetorical and a moron."

"Thank you, Dad."

"Well, can we know who this little tramp is you've found?" Mick bursts out.

"It's me."

Fred and Mick are stunned. They lean forward. They had almost forgotten the mousey secretary standing behind Julian and yet it is she who has spoken. She takes a step forward and confirms with dignity, "I'm the woman that Julian has fallen for. We're going to get married as soon as he gets a divorce."

"Precisely," Julian says.

Open-mouthed, taken aback, Fred and Mick look at her and can find no words to say.

The woman steps up next to Julian. They clasp each other.

He looks wonderful, as handsome as George Clooney. She looks the opposite.

"And who the bloody hell are you anyway?"

"My name is Paloma Faith. And I'm not a little tramp, I'm a singer."

"We work together. I'm producing her next album," Julian explains proudly.

Mick manages to scrape some rationality together and says to the woman, "Would you mind leaving us a moment? My daughter-in-law's father and I would like a word in private with my son here."

"Alright, but not for very long. We can't bear to separated from each other for more than five minutes."

"Very kind of you, my dear, but you needn't worry, I only need a minute to understand my son's thinking."

The woman goes off with an awkward and graceless gait. Fred and Mick follow her with their eyes and wait until she is out of the room. At that point they look up to meet Julian's self-satisfied and composed face.

Mick seems sincere. He really wants to fathom what makes human beings tick. "I'm sorry, Julian, but I really want to get this. It may be unimaginative of me perhaps, I may also be old and incapable of understanding, but you really have to explain this to me: Lena's a very beautiful woman, a dream. This creature here's the most insignificant woman on earth. Basically, what I mean is, what the bloody hell do you see in her?"

For the first time Julian is uncomfortable. He sighs. He looks to one side. "You really want to know?"

"Yes, I really want to know."

Julian takes his time. He checks to see that the woman is no longer in the room, then he turns to look at his father and says all in one breath, "Well, to be honest, she's really good in bed."

Now Mick and Fred really cannot find anything more to say.

21

Fred and Lena are walking along that beautiful valley.

She is dignified and serious, staring into space.

He is ill at ease and has no idea what to say to her. Then he is distracted by a bird that suddenly breaks into song, until Lena brings him back to reality.

"So who is this shitty woman?"

"Someone called Paloma Faith."

"And what does she do with herself?"

"The most obscene profession in the world."

"What? A prostitute?"

"Worse. A pop star."

"And what did Julian say?"

"I've already told you."

"You haven't told me a thing, actually. You've mumbled a few disconnected words."

"That's because he was mumbling. He's not right in the head."

"Well, I disagree. I think his head knows exactly what it's doing. He's made twenty decisions in a couple of hours. He's left home. He's rented an apartment. He's spoken to the lawyer about a divorce. He doesn't seem to have lost it to me. You say this woman's ugly and insignificant, so what does he see in her that he doesn't in me?"

"How should I know?"

"But you said that Mick had asked him."

"I did?"

"Yes, you did. And what did he say?"

"You know, I don't remember."

"You're beginning to really piss me off, Pa. You know very well what he said, and you're hopeless at lying. Tell me what he said."

"I really don't remember. He would have mumbled some idiocy or other."

"If you don't tell me I'll start screaming right here and now. What did he say? What in hell's name has this woman got – for him – that I don't have? I want to know. What did Julian say? I want to know."

Fred stops in his tracks. He has reached his limit and decides to satisfy her. "He said she's good in bed."

Lena is dumbstruck. Her face is pinched, she looks furious. With a cold ferocity she says to her father, "You didn't actually have to tell me that, Pa."

She sets off at a swift pace, leaving her father alone in the middle of the valley, while the two notes the boy was practising start playing in his head, not on the violin but rather on a sullen bassoon.

*

In the midst of all the steam from the saunas and the Turkish baths, naked bodies of all ages appear dead in the half-light, abandoned in the heat and sweat.

Bodies toned and gleaming, bodies large and round, ancient bodies falling to pieces. This is what the effort to be healthy looks like. This is how some people try to prolong the future or awkwardly try to pursue the youthful past.

And then there are the outlines of human beings buried with their eyes closed in bathtubs under compresses of warm, fresh hay, like living meadows, stationary still lifes, while the bassoon plays at a discreet volume without ever deviating from those two simple notes.

22

Candles, incense and subdued lighting.

Fred and Lena are stretched out naked on marble tables on their backs, completely covered in compresses of dark mud. They seem like two figures left petrified after a volcanic eruption. Only their eyes are free of mud and they stare lifelessly at the ceiling across which dull soft lights play hypnotically.

A little clumsily, Fred tries to act the father. "I do understand you, Lena. I really do, believe me."

Lena remains silent. But later, when she does reply, she speaks clearly, angrily and without mercy. "You do understand me, do you, Pa? Like hell you do! My mother would have understood me. My mother, who found herself in the state I'm now in dozens of times. And pretended not to notice. You've been with dozens and dozens of women and she simply had to cope with it and get by. Not only for us children, but also – and above all – for you. She loved you and forgave you. She wanted to stay with you no matter what. But who did she want to stay with? I mean, who? That's what I asked her. A man who never gave anything in return, that's who. You never gave a thing. To her, to me – nothing. You gave yourself to your music, that's what. There was nothing else in your life. Only music. And a lack of feeling. Never a touch, a hug, a kiss – nothing. You've never known anything about your children, if they were upset or were happy. Nothing. Everything was on my mother's shoulders. You only said three words to her at home: 'Melanie, quiet, please.' And she had to tell us, 'Quiet, your father's composing', 'Be quiet, your father's resting before his concert tonight', 'Be quiet, your father's resting after his concert', 'Be quiet, your father's talking to someone important on the telephone', 'Be quiet, Stravinsky's coming to visit your father today.' You wanted to be like Stravinsky, only you didn't have the tiniest bit of his genius. 'Quiet, please, Melanie!' That's all you knew how to say. You never knew a thing about my mother. You never cared one bit about what she went through. And even now, it's been ten years since you took her any flowers. And as for that letter! Do you think she never read it? Well, you're wrong. She found it and she read it. And I found it, too. Perhaps you don't even remember it, but we do. The letter in which you declared your love for another man. My mother had to endure that humiliation as well. 'My necessary sexual experiments . . .' That's what you said. Musical experiments weren't enough for you, you had to try out homosexual ones as well! You didn't give a fuck about my mother's suffering. So don't come to me and say you understand, because you don't understand anything for shit."

She ends there. Fred says not a word. They remain buried in the mud, staring at the ceiling.

23

One wall of the hotel's huge gym is set up for free climbing.

The hippy mountaineer has reached the top of the wall, eight metres above the ground. And he seems admirably nonchalant as he hangs by one hand in empty space with no ropes to support him. He then turns to the pallid thirteen-year-old who has remained at the foot of the wall. She has not climbed one centimetre.

From the summit, the man says to her gently, "Come on, Frances, have a go."

The girl looks up at him from below and says nothing, just chews on her fingernails.

"Wouldn't you like to see what the world looks like from up here?"

The girl peers up at him again and nods.

"Good, then have a go."

She shakes her head.

"O.K., well, wait there." With three swift movements, the mountaineer is back on the ground.

"Get up on my shoulders."

The girl clambers on the enormous man's shoulders. With the same nonchalance, he climbs back up the wall without any effort, as if it were a little rucksack were on his shoulders not a human being.

"Now while we're climbing you can look down. See how beautiful the world is from up here."

Clinging to the man's shoulders, the girl turns and looks down. She sees a figure watching them from the gym door. It is Lena.

The girl taps the man's shoulder as if to invite him to look down as well. He turns and glances down, but Lena is no longer there. She has left the gym.

24

Another garden in the hotel, more isolated and remote, borders on an outbuilding where the staff are housed. No hotel guests go near the place. The main complex seems miles away. In the middle of the garden luxuriant roses grow among miniature fountains and an artificial stream. Everything arranged to create an inelegant version of a lyrical, flowery Eden.

No guests ever go there? Well, actually one guest does and that guest is Fred Ballinger. He is sitting on a bench in the middle of the garden, staring at the artificial stream, sucking on a sweet. His eyes are so full of sadness it would be difficult to imagine they could bear any more. He seems to be in a trance, absent, totally absorbed. But he suddenly rouses himself and takes out his handkerchief. He blows into it and then rapidly wipes his nose four times before folding it and putting it back in his pocket.

As he puts the handkerchief away his attention is caught by what he can see through the window on the ground floor of the staff's lodgings. He can see the outline of the petite shy masseuse now wearing a T-shirt and shorts, her supple movements suggesting she is dancing. In fact, she is bouncing around in front of a video screen playing an Xbox game. A stylised female figure in the video invites her to copy her movements.

It is wonderfully poignant to see this tiny girl playing virtual tennis with such unusual determination: sweating, her hair plastered to her forehead and temples.

Fred watches her with one hand instinctively rubbing the sweet wrapper in a musical rhythm.

He is unaware that another figure in a white dressing gown is standing behind him also watching the girl as she plays. It is the American actor, Jimmy Tree.

25

Many people are having dinner. Again, there is an unearthly silence.

Fred and Mick are staring at the silent German couple, as ever wearing matching colours; today it is shades of blue.

Lena enters the room. She has abandoned her sober and simple look, and to go with her new elegant hairstyle she has decided to wear quite a provocative dress.

Mick feels a twinge of nostalgia. "You remind me of Brenda Morel aged thirty, when she was filming 'At Home with James' with me. You should always dress like this, Lena."

"From now on that's exactly what I intend to do."

Fred follows her with his gaze, but she deliberately avoids looking at him as she sits down next to them.

From another table the hippy mountaineer cannot help noticing how beautiful Lena is. His eyes light up, but then the sparkle goes out in them as if he is already overcome by a sense of defeat before he has even started. Dispirited, he lets his spoon drop onto his plate and cannot eat another thing.

Jimmy is at his table with Mark Kozelek and other friends. They are all talking among themselves in pairs, except for Jimmy who is trying to figure out what is happening between the mountaineer and Lena, anxious not to miss a single detail.

Then, out of the silence, something extraordinary happens.

The silent German woman gets calmly to her feet and, with sudden violence, lands a slap on her husband's face. The man all but tumbles from his chair.

Needless to say, everyone turns round to look at them, astounded.

With great dignity, the woman turns and leaves the room.

Stock still, Mick, Fred and Lena follow the proceedings with open mouths.

The group around the actor's table starts to snigger furtively, but not Jimmy Tree. He is also amazed.

The slapped husband pays not the slightest attention to everyone looking at him and calmly goes back to eating his mushroom velouté.

Supported by his wife, the South American leaves his table and crosses the room with great effort to get to the exit. But when he gets to the man who was slapped he decides to stop. The elderly German looks up at him and the South American does two things: first he gives the man a gentle smile and then with his podgy hand he caresses his cheek. The elderly man now has a look of gratitude on his face and attempts to return the smile.

Then the South American hobbles off in the ensuing funereal silence.

Jimmy Tree has, of course, followed everything and is starting to feel emotional.

26

In the garden opposite the swimming pool the usual stage has been erected. This evening a local singer is performing, accompanied by three musicians. She is an elegant woman in her fifties.

Dotted about the seats, people are following the excellent performance with interest.

Fred, Mick and Lena are sitting at one of the small tables, quietly listening to the woman giving a wonderful rendition of "Lili Marlene".

His face devoid of any expression, Jimmy Tree stands to hear the song. He is serious, concentrating, whispering the words of the song in German. He knows them off by heart.

Then he senses a presence to his left. He turns round. The silent German woman is staring at him with one hand held out as if inviting him to dance. He smiles and goes up to her. They start the slow dance.

The woman's husband, sitting at another little table, is a mass of seething rage, consumed by jealousy.

Intrigued, Fred and Mick stare at the actor and the woman as they continue to dance.

Jimmy whispers in the woman's ear by way of observation, without any intention to seduce, "Did you know that's a wonderful perfume you're wearing?"

From a distance Mick and Fred are waiting for the woman to say something.

Embarrassed, she makes no reply, but clings to him a little more tightly. Jimmy also holds her more closely and while he dances he closes his eyes and lets himself drift away. From their table, Kozelek and his friends look on with intense expressions.

The hippy mountaineer clumsily pretends to walk past Fred and Mick, but it is obvious he is making a tortuous detour only to catch sight of Lena. She does not even notice him. Despite being an expert mountaineer, in his anxiety he trips up on a table leg, but manages not to fall.

"Lili Marlene" comes to an end. The German woman beams at Jimmy, who smiles back. They break up from the dance.

She goes back to her husband. He glares at her. She avoids his gaze.

Jimmy Tree sits himself down next to Fred with a tisane. They exchange a knowing look, plainly revealing the sympathy they have for one another.

"Is that a simple tisane or is it laced with gin and tonic?"

"Simple one. I'm trying to be a good boy."

Fred smiles. "What a pity!"

He blows his nose in his usual fashion. Jimmy watches.

"How's work coming along on your character?" Fred asks.

"Well . . . not bad. I've found some interesting details."

"Excellent."

"This morning, that girl who was dancing by herself. I saw her as well. It was something . . . well, it was something . . ."

". . . Unforgettable."

"That's it. That's exactly the right word. Unforgettable."

Jimmy finishes his tisane and takes his leave with his usual playful military salute. Fred grins at him, but Lena quickly wipes the smile off his face.

"Perhaps the problem is that Julian and I never had children."

Fred turns to look at her. His tone is serious. "I don't know what the problem is. And I'm not going to try and boost your morale by telling you lies or things I've never understood. You're right: music is all I understand. And do you know why I understand it? Because music doesn't need words or experience. It is what it is. Your mother would have understood you. Not me. But your mother's not here."

They look at each other, but say not another word.

The elegant chanteuse of "Lili Marlene", with her aristocratic, old-fashioned profile, is the only presence in the deserted restaurant. She is sitting at a random table, in her evening dress, with her eyes lowered, as she devours a chicken leg held between her fingers, concentrating on it like a ravenous beast. Suddenly, she stops. She looks up into empty space, a fixed and stern expression on her face, and in that precise moment a line of the "Lili Marlene" she sang echoes unaccompanied in her mind. Her gaze falls on the chicken leg and the song comes to an end. She starts eating again with the same voracity as before.

It is late. There is no longer anyone in the garden where they hold the concerts, except for Fred Ballinger who has fallen asleep in one of the chairs. The lights are low. He opens his eyes and sees a dozen swing seats spread about the garden moving in unison to the breeze. Everything else is still.

The hotel lobby is empty but for one figure sitting on a couch: the young dumpy escort girl, just as ill at ease as before.

Mick Boyle walks across the lobby. He is going to his room for the night. He spots the girl. She gives him a gauche nod and a wink.

He smiles at her, but the smile is a fatherly one that signifies a gentle refusal. He walks on.

The girl looks serious and sad again, but after a few metres Mick stops, as if he has had second thoughts.

The girl has noticed he has stopped, but deliberately keeps her eyes off him.

Mick turns towards her. He is tempted. He stares at the girl and reflects a moment.

She then decides to catch his eye, but it is too late. Mick has gone.

27

Fred and Lena are asleep in the double bed.

Outside, behind the windows, a theatrical light slowly appears on the balcony and illuminates ten female figures dressed in black. All are motionless and severe.

At the same time, gradually, comes the sound of a violin with the first notes of "Simple Song, Number 3".

The ten women join the violin and start to sing beautifully in soprano voices.

Fred opens his eyes and says, "That's enough."

Then, all of a sudden, like someone possessed, he throws off the covers and hurls himself against the window. But there is no-one on the balcony. It is empty and dark. Fred punches the glass violently and screams, "That's enough! Stop singing right now. Enough."

Lena wakes up with a start. She is worried. "That's enough yourself, Pa. Stop now. You were dreaming."

Fred comes to his senses. He stops screaming and stays there as if hanging against the glass, lost. Lena looks at him from behind, but now has nothing to say.

28

Several paragliders are circling silently just below the angular peaks of the mountains.

Fred and Mick are on a walk.

Out of the blue, and a little theatrically, as if fishing around for any old subject, Fred says, "I had a very long piss this morning. A powerful one. And while I was having it, I was thinking, 'Heavens, when's it going to end? When's it going to end?' And it never seemed to end. And I was so happy. I haven't been that happy for months."

Mick hides his displeasure. "Great. I'm very happy for you."

But Fred notices his friend is suffering from what he has said. 'I'm only joking, Mick. Nothing like that happened."

"Don't joke about these things, Fred. The prostate's a serious thing."

"But you always fall for it. For sixty years now you've believed everything I tell you."

"I create stories and in order to do so I have to believe in everything. You remember the other day? When you told me you couldn't remember your parents anymore?"

Fred laughs. "No, I don't remember."

"Of course you do, you do remember. You made me think that not only do I not remember my parents, but almost nothing of my childhood. There's only one thing I do remember."

"What's that?"

"The exact moment I learned to ride a bicycle. It may be nothing, but what a joy! A real joy! And this morning for the first time, as if by magic, I also remembered what happened next."

"You fell off."

"How the hell did you know that?"

"Because that's what happens to everyone, Mick. You learn how to do the thing, you feel great, and then you forget to brake."

"But isn't that a great metaphor for life?"

"Let's not draw hasty conclusions, Mick."

And then a magical thing happens. An eleven-year-old boy is coming down the mountainside in the opposite direction on a mountain bike, pedalling along with amazing skill, and with one wheel raised. Mick and Fred are transfixed, speechless. The boy continues to do the whole stretch on a single wheel and passes them by at top speed, silent as a ghost.

The two friends turn to stare after him, enchanted.

Fred reflects a moment and then says, "You know something, Mick?"

"What's that?"

"You and me, I don't think we'll ever die."

Mick turns to face his friend. He smiles at him and adds,

"Now let's not draw hasty conclusions, Fred!"

But then something else grabs his attention: he catches sight of the silent couple of sixty-year-old Germans as they are about to enter the thick woodland, dressed in matching green. He makes a sign to Fred, who turns and sees the couple disappearing into the wood as well. Fred has no hesitation. He beckons to Mick.

"Let's follow them."

29

Fred and Mick are crouching quietly behind a bramble bush, looking at something. And what do they see?

They see the couple of sixty-year-olds up against a tree. Their clothes pushed aside as best they can, the man is penetrating the woman with the vigour of a sex-starved adolescent.

They are going at it like crazy. The man is in a frenzy. The woman is approaching climax. Then they both come together. In unison. The legendary simultaneous orgasm, both of them crying out with pleasure.

In their own way, they have spoken.

Without betraying any emotion, Fred takes out his wallet and hands Mick fifty francs.

30

Fred is walking down a corridor.

Lena is waiting for him at the door to their suite.

She seems agitated, breathless, anxious to speak to her father, and lets him know it immediately. "Where have you been, Pa? A man's been waiting here for you for an hour. He says he's an emissary from the Queen."

Fred snorts, as if the visit is unwelcome.

"I've had him wait in the little lounge."

31

Lena pours the emissary a coffee. The two men sit opposite one another separated by the coffee table, the man on a couch and Fred in a small armchair. Lena then goes to sit in a chair behind her father.

The royal agent drums his fingers nervously on his trouser pocket, the outline of a cigarette packet clearly visible under the fabric. Fred notices.

"You can smoke here, if you like."

The emissary cannot believe his ears. He is overcome, as if there has just been an earthquake. "How is that possible?"

"The hotel manager is mad about music and for that reason I enjoy a few small privileges."

The other man gives him a smile of infinite gratitude. "You don't know what pleasure this gives me."

"Are you feeling tense?"

"Very tense," the man says as he inhales a deep restorative drag on the cigarette.

"There's no ashtray though."

"It doesn't matter. I'll make do."

"So, tell me everything, because I don't have much time. In a short while I have to have a colonic irrigation, cleaning out my intestine."

Instinctively the emissary pulls a strained face and adds, "Is it a painful operation?"

"No, just embarrassing."

The man gives a sigh and starts to speak. "I haven't been able to convince the Queen. I mentioned your reservations about the songs, so I proposed an alternative programme. A different composer. A completely different evening. She wouldn't hear of it. There was nothing to be done. She wants you and only you and your 'Simple Songs'. She says Prince Philip won't countenance anything else."

"I'm sorry. I don't wish to appear rude. But this isn't going to happen."

"But why?"

"I already explained the last time we met. The reasons are personal."

"And there's no way of resolving these personal reasons?"

"Unfortunately not."

"What I'm actually doing is begging you. My job is not an easy one. I have to return to London with a positive answer."

"I'm sorry, but the answer's no."

Lena is following the conversation attentively.

"I don't follow. What is it you don't like? The date? The place? The orchestra? The soprano? The Queen?"

"Please, don't insist. The reasons are personal."

The emissary loses some of his patience and his capacity for diplomacy. "So what are these blessed personal reasons?"

Fred does not reply.

Lena begins to understand. We have no idea what Fred means, but she does. And without letting herself be seen, she starts sobbing silently.

"If the reasons are personal it's because the person isn't prepared to say."

"Help me to resolve these personal problems. What is it that's not right?"

Fred says, at random: "The soprano."

The emissary beams. He thinks he has found the solution. "Then we'll change her. No problem."

"There'd be no point."

"Even though Sumi Jo is the greatest of all sopranos and has said she's very keen to be directed by you? I said very keen? She was over the moon."

"I'm not interested."

"What do you have against her?"

"Nothing at all! I don't even know her."

"Well then?"

For the first time Fred loses his patience. He raises his voice, almost shouting. "That's enough! Enough!"

Lena is now crying a little more, her eyes full of tears. She tries to hide the fact.

The emissary notices and cannot understand. He falls silent. He has no idea what to say. He throws his arms out wide, defeated. "I really don't understand. What is the problem?"

Fred shouts again, the words coming out in a stream, without thinking. "The problem is that 'Simple Songs' were composed for my wife. And only my wife has sung them. Only my wife has recorded them. And as long as I'm alive only my wife will sing them. But the problem, my dear sir, is that my wife can no longer sing them. Have you now understood? Have you?"

Lena has put her hands over her face to stop her tears. Fred seems exhausted, beside himself.

The emissary has nothing left to say. He gets to his feet, stubbing the cigarette out in the packet. In dismay, he replies, "Yes, I understand now, and from the bottom of my heart ask you to forgive me."

Very quickly he makes for the exit.

Fred and Lena remain as they are. He is staring into space, she is in tears behind him.

Down the corridors, the little bells start to tinkle merrily.

On the footbridge where the members of staff go to smoke, they all extinguish their cigarettes and, like a flock of sheep being rounded up, return to the hotel and go back to work.

32

The young masseuse pours oil over her hands.

Lying on his stomach on the massage table, his head set in the face hole, Fred is looking down at the floor where he can see a woman's tiny sandals.

The girl gently spreads her palms on Fred's naked back and starts to massage, but shortly afterwards she stops.

"I'm going to try a different kind of massage. I can see you're stressed. Or rather, no, it's not stress. You're upset."

"You can tell this from your hands?"

"You can tell a lot of things by touch. But people are frightened of being touched. I'm not sure why."

"Perhaps because they think it's only a question of pleasure."

"Well, that's another reason why people should touch rather than talk."

Fred remains silent. He stares at the floor. After a while he says, "You don't enjoy talking?"

"I never have anything to say," she admits.

"We sometimes forget, but sincerity's a wonderful thing, isn't it?"

The masseuse has changed to a different style of massage. She has nothing more to say.

Fred shuts his eyes and relaxes.

33

Mick and his scriptwriters are walking up a steep path towards the top of a mountain.

They meet a young family on their way down. The father is carrying his three-year-old son in a baby backpack carrier and the boy is sleeping beatifically. Mick studies the child.

Mick and his scriptwriters reach the summit with its wonderful views, a place to enjoy the silence floating in the clean air and appreciate the magnificent vista of the Alpine peaks and valleys.

There is a coin-operated telescope for tourists.

The little group observes the view in silence. Mick moves away from them and slips a coin into the telescope.

Then he calls to the youngsters, "Come and look at this."

The girl is first. Mick shows her how it works, while the others stand by. "Now listen. You see that mountain opposite?"

"Yes, it seems very near."

"Precisely. This is what you see when you're young. You see everything up close. And that's the future. Now look this way."

He takes her hand and invites her to look through the opposite end of the telescope.

The girl sees the faces of her young friends in the reverse view. Although only two metres from her, they seem far away.

"And that's the way you see things when you're old. Everything's distant. That's the past."

The girl is moved. She cannot see – because everything is too distant in the reverse view – that the young man she is always arguing with is also moved.

They all fall silent.

Mick goes over to a bag, crouches down and extracts a bottle of spumante and some plastic glasses while he explains, "As a boy I said to myself, if I get to be old I mustn't make the same mistake all old people make: they become boring and pedantic. But that's exactly what I've become. So, please excuse me. Now let's turn to serious concerns: I'm so proud to have written this script with you, and Brenda can't wait to start. And I have to confess something to you. I've made twenty films, but they're all irrelevant now. At this point, only this film makes any sense to me. In it . . . well, yes, it's going to be my lasting testimony: emotional, intellectual and moral. This is the only film for me. Nothing else. So let's drink a toast to finishing the third draft of 'Last Day in a Life'."

"And the final scene, Mick?"

"We'll find it sooner or later. Chin-chin!"

There is no-one in the picturesque garden with its age-old trees and covered pathways until a thickset man with a gigantic stomach appears ready for a massage, completely covered in mud. He looks like a statue gone wrong. Extremely pissed off, he is screaming into the cell phone in his hand in an Italian betraying a strong Neapolitan accent. "Bebè, I hope you realise you're asking me to deliver 24,000 *mozzarelle* in two days? You know you're on another planet here? Now listen to me carefully: don't start stressing me out while I'm relaxing on holiday. The last person to upset me on holiday can't relax himself anymore . . . *Ciao*. I'll write you on WhatsApp tomorrow."

34

Jimmy Tree and Fred Ballinger are floating quietly in the swimming pool. Side by side, with their shoulders against the wall of the pool, they let themselves be rocked by a powerful jet of water along the spine.

Fred opens an eye and glimpses Mick not far away as he walks along with the doctor. They are deep in conversation. Fred closes his eyes.

The two bathers remain silent, eyes closed, until the arrival of the boy violinist rouses them.

"Hello, Fred Ballinger."

"*Ciao.*"

"I wanted to say that I went and checked at reception and you actually are Fred Ballinger."

"Good, I'm glad you're now satisfied."

Jimmy Tree smiles.

"I wanted to tell you something else."

"Please do."

"I wanted to say that since you corrected the position of my elbow I find it much easier to play. The sound comes out more naturally."

"Excellent. And do you know why? Because you're left-handed. Left-handers have difficulty keeping things even and an uneven position actually helps them."

Out of the blue, the South American's bloated face appears. He has heard the conversation and, betraying a strong Spanish accent, he innocently confesses to the three, "I am left-handed as well."

Fred, Jimmy and the boy look at him, stunned.

Jimmy gives him a great smile and tells him, "Jesus Christ, the whole world knows that!"

35

Lena is sitting by the side of the hotel's pleasant little lake wearing nothing but a towel. With her wet hair spread over her shoulders she appears even more beautiful than she is.

Opposite her, brimming with emotion, sits the hippy mountaineer. Also wearing nothing but a towel, he seems like a huge bear. Hirsute shoulders and chest, beard, long hair – a truly huge but peaceful beast.

She keeps her eyes closed. He cannot take his kindly eyes off her.

He swallows, plucks up courage, is about to speak, then shyness prevails, until he decides to try again. This is his moment. He starts to speak in a heavy Tyrolean accent. "My name is Lucio. Lucio Moroder."

And in his embarrassment he gives out an idiotic laugh that rumbles like thunder.

Lena opens her eyes and with no expression in her voice, confines herself to a sterile "Hi".

"I am a mountaineer. Also an instructor. I give lessons here at the hotel." He gives another idiotic laugh that raises doubts about his level of intelligence. "This watch is a Forerunner 620 with colour touchscreen display. It can give a VO_2 max estimate, which is the maximum capacity to consume oxygen during maximum stress. I want to give it to my cousin for Christmas. We always climb together. He should have been here, but he slipped in the bath and broke his femur."

Lena gives him a polite smile. "Yes, a bathtub's more dangerous than Everest."

"This is a very accurate observation." The mountaineer pauses for a moment. "Do you know what I once found on the summit of K2?"

"No, what?"

"A bedside table."

"You're kidding."

"No, it's true. I opened it and there was nothing in it." After another pause, he starts again. "You feel a wonderful sensation when you climb, you know? A real feeling of freedom."

He again laughs like a simpleton, as if he never knows how to follow up on what he says.

Lena closes her eyes and again makes a vaguely ironic comment. "I'd only feel fear."

"That's also a wonderful feeling, you know?" And, once more, he laughs like an idiot.

Lena opens her eyes, but does not look at him.

The little lake is overlooked by a glass cube that holds the indoor swimming pool. Above them, on the other side of the glass, an expressionless Fred Ballinger stands watching his daughter below.

36

Fred, Mick and Jimmy Tree are peacefully sunning themselves on loungers, wrapped in white dressing gowns. All have their eyes closed.

Fred has a newspaper open on his lap. Mick and Jimmy are chatting.

"Who's the most talented actress you've ever worked with, Mr Boyle?"

"Brenda Morel. No doubt about it. She's a genius. She may not have read more than two books in her whole life, and one of those was her autobiography – which a ghostwriter wrote for her, of course – but Brenda remains a genius."

Jimmy sniggers. "In what sense is she a genius?"

"If you know how to steal, you don't need to be educated. Theft is your education. That's how Brenda is. Even when she became a star – thanks to my films – she never forgot that her home was on the streets. And that's where she's stayed, on the streets, where she steals everything she sees. Everything. That's how she created those memorable characters. And won two Oscars."

"What did she steal?"

"We're shooting 'The Crystal Woman'. In one scene, at the back of the film set, an electrician with a slight limp goes past, making an almost imperceptible sound when he steps on his shorter leg. No-one had heard it, but she did. So while she's playing the part, she stops and calls 'Cut'. I shout, 'Brenda, what the hell . . . ? I'm the only one to call cut.' 'Like hell, Mick,' she says. 'If we're getting the character wrong, I call cut.' She's looking at the electrician. The guy wants to sink into the ground, but she lights up and says, 'Mick, my character should have one leg shorter than the other. She walks with a limp.' I fall off my chair and tell her, 'Brenda, are you crazy? Your character can't have a limp. Your character is a woman the whole world desires, every man wants to go to bed with her, she's a dream.' And she says, 'Mick, even dreams have problems.'" Jimmy laughs. "She was right. With that little trick she won her second Oscar."

A dull intermittent sound that only Fred hears at first forces him to open his eyes. But the sun is shining directly at them, so all he can see is a small black disc that sails into view against the sky from below and then falls down again. Then again the sound and again the black disc sails into view.

It is enough to make Fred curious and decide to take a look. He sets off and Jimmy and Mick Boyle follow him.

37

When they get to the tennis court Fred, Mick and Jimmy are struck dumb by what they see.

With tremendous effort, the overweight South American is doing something extraordinary: with his left foot he launches a tennis ball to a great height, and then without letting it touch the ground when it falls, he kicks it back up again twenty metres or so into the air. A yellow tennis ball against the sky.

It plummets down and he kicks it back up again with a natural skill that both impresses and elicits admiration.

Mick, Jimmy and Fred cannot believe their eyes. And not without reason.

Then, after five or six of these acrobatic miracles, the man is tired out and stops. He is struggling for breath.

Jimmy locates the briarwood walking stick leaning against the wire-mesh fence. He fetches it and quickly takes it over.

The South American is extremely grateful. He is dripping with sweat, and without saying a word sets off walking slowly with his stick.

Jimmy, Fred and Mick remain rooted there, standing on the tennis court watching the world's most talented retired footballer as he battles to leave the field.

38

English-style flowered wallpaper. Beside the wall, as on every afternoon, a small table holds a splendid silver tea service.

A woman's handbag smashes into the tea service. Everything ends up on the floor. As it falls, the handbag opens. It contains nothing.

After a second, disturbed by the event, the Queen's emissary manages to say in a feeble voice, "Your Majesty, you almost hit me!"

"Yes, Mr Bale, I meant to almost hit you."

The emissary sighs with exhaustion, as if the whole universe were going to hell in handbags.

39

At dinner, the German couple is silent once more. They eat with composure, looking elsewhere.

The hippy mountaineer is disconsolate, his hopes dashed as he eyes Lena, who sits at a table with Fred and Mick, paying him no attention.

Jimmy Tree is dining with Mark Kozelek and other friends. They are laughing at the actor, who is doing a perfect impression of Marlon Brando.

The evening meal is sushi. Everyone is eating with chopsticks.

Fred, Mick and Lena are eating in silence.

As usual Lena has a message to pass on. "The French called again. They keep on about that book of memoirs . . . your work, your life. What should I say?"

Her father reflects. "Tell them . . ." Then he has no idea what else to say. Silence. Lena and Mick wait for him.

"Well, what?" Lena asks.

"To forget me! Tell them that. I'm retired. Out of it. From work and from life."

Mick raises his eyes to heaven, as if he has heard this same old song too many times and is sick of it.

"I've got nothing to say, and more than anything else, I'm just not interested," Fred continues.

"Can you give over with this bullshit? You and your music have managed to communicate completely new emotions."

"But, Mick, the emotions are overrated."

Mick throws his chopsticks down on the table. He is pissed off. "When you put on the garb of the depressive cynic you're unbearable. How I've managed to stay friends with you all these years is a real mystery."

"You're a patient man, Mick."

"And you're an idiot."

"Some truth in that!"

Lena is about to make a comment, but in his anger Mick gets in before her. "A book on your work, about what you've experienced, will be there for ever. It'll help young musicians – everyone. It's important—"

Fred interrupts him. "Yes, it's important . . . You have to leave a memento for future generations, hand your knowledge down . . . I've heard the same old story for years . . . but they're just a feeble excuse, Mick, a means of pretending not to see the one great problem."

"And what's the one great problem?"

"Death, Mick! Death. Lurking just around the corner."

"Yes, and while you're thinking about death lurking round the corner, you forget to live. Even while you're alive." Mick nods vigorously as he turns to Lena. "You know why he pisses me off?"

"Yes, she does know why," Fred replies.

"But doesn't running through your life and work again hold any fascination for you?" his daughter asks.

"No. It makes me feel ill. Can't you two understand that? Besides, there's nothing to say. Stravinsky said it all. He started to compose simple music and they all attacked him. 'Sacrilege', they said. 'He's deserted Modernism', the critics thundered. But he was only rediscovering the past and its mirror. And then he said to them this wonderful thing: 'You *respect*, but I love.' What can I add to that?"

Lena and Mick say nothing more. Fred picks up his chopsticks again and holds them in mid-air without eating. Lena stares at him.

Completely unexpectedly, the boy who plays the violin approaches. Fred does not even notice him.

With great delicacy, the boy moves the hand that holds the chopsticks by three centimetres, as if to correct its position. Fred raises his eyes and gives him a mournful smile.

The boy smiles back at him and then nothing more. He runs off, as all children do, needing to keep on the move all the time.

40

On the stage in the hotel garden, a fakir is lying on a bed of nails.

At a table, Lena, Fred, Mick and Jimmy Tree are watching. "These performances are really depressing," Jimmy says. "All we need now is the mime artist."

"He usually come towards the end of the season," Fred says.

The fakir rises in one piece from his bed of nails. Applause from the audience.

His back is red raw as he exhales fire from his mouth. Then he says, "Thank you all. Now please continue to enjoy the evening with the traditional ensemble of Alpine horns."

Eight elderly men with immensely long horns come onto the stage and try to breathe some life into a lugubrious and monotonous piece.

A man who could be assumed to be the hotel manager comes up to the table and addresses Jimmy Tree, but Fred, Mick and Lena listen in to the conversation.

"Excuse me, Mr Tree, but we have a new guest in the hotel.

Her name is Joyce Owens. She has just won the title of Miss Universe. She is a great admirer of yours and would very much like to meet you."

"O.K., fine with that."

The manager makes a sign and out of a dark corner of the garden appears Miss Universe.

They all wait for her in a state of excitement, but Miss Universe is an outright disappointment. She is wearing a cheap baggy jumpsuit that distorts her figure, making her seem overweight. She has bad skin, tired and unwashed hair and, although it is dark, is wearing purple-tinted sunglasses in vulgar frames that appear too large for her face. In addition, she has a grating voice when she shakes Jimmy's hand.

"Pleased to meet you. I'm a huge fan of yours. I literally went crazy for you when you played that Mr Q."

Jimmy Tree raises his eyes to heaven. He can take no more of Mr Q.

"I go to see all the Transformers films, but that one's my favourite."

"Thank you. And do you go to see any films that aren't about robots?" he asks sarcastically.

"Of course! I've got my whole life ahead of me and I want to become an actress. I don't want to get stuck in the beauty business."

Jimmy sniggers. "And what else do you go to see? Cartoons?"

Miss Universe stiffens a little. "I go and see whatever I want."

"Excellent, Miss Universe."

She now becomes very serious. "Do you know something, Mr Tree?"

"What's that?"

"I like irony, but when it's full of venom it loses its potency and reveals something else."

"Oh, so what does it reveal? Let's hear it."

"Frustration. In this case yours, not mine."

Jimmy stiffens. "Me? Frustrated, Miss Universe?"

"I'm happy to have participated in Miss Universe, but are you happy to have played Mr Q?"

The actor has no answer to this.

A feeling of embarrassment has fallen over the gathering.

Jimmy holds out his hand to Miss Universe, almost as if admitting defeat. She does not shake it and leaves.

Boyle smoothes his hair down with the palm of his hand and Jimmy watches him. Then, to break the ice as his eyes follow the rapidly disappearing Miss Universe, he says, "The arrogance of youth is intolerable."

"Especially if those who witness it are no longer young," Fred adds.

Mick laughs and says, "That woman should be stabbed to death, believe me. Stabbed to death."

Fred turns to Jimmy, who is once more listening to the alpenhorns and remarks drily, "She's no fool, that Miss Universe."

"No way, for sure!" Jimmy replies, without looking at him.

They both break out in large grins.

Lena watches Miss Universe leave with that look women have when they observe other women and, when the model is out of sight, she turns and deliberately fixes her eyes on the hippy mountaineer, who – naturally – is staring only at her. His eyes start to gleam as they never have before.

41

A deluxe Maserati is speeding along a sunny mountain road. Julian is at the wheel. Paloma Faith pops up from the back seat wearing splendid make-up. She is singing a funky number that would have even a corpse dancing. Dressed in skimpy lingerie, she writhes about sinuously and sensually. A complete about-turn from the dull colourless woman who first appeared at the hotel. She licks Julian's ear with the tip of her tongue and he moans with pleasure. Paloma moves about the car's interior on all fours like a panther in a crescendo of throbbing eroticism. Still singing, she slides lithely out of the open car window like a snake.

She climbs onto the roof and stands up and sings and dances there without ever losing her sensuality.

Because this is evidently the fantasy sequence of a video clip she does not fall from the moving car.

Julian leans out of the window and looks up at her, excited, burbling like an idiot. He leans out so far to grasp Paloma that he is forced to steer the car with one foot. The car swerves, but there is no danger. This is a video clip.

Julian gets back into his seat to avoid an accident. He looks at the road, but not for long because now Paloma appears on the outside of the windscreen.

She is sliding slowly down onto the car bonnet. With her body pressed against the glass, she winks, making eyes at him, showing her tongue and everything else as she rolls around with the wind in her hair and the car still speeding along at 200 kilometres an hour.

Finally, with an acrobatic movement, Paloma gets back inside the car again through the side window.

She sits beside Julian. He wants to touch her, but she knows to stop him in order to prolong the pleasure.

Meanwhile, she continues singing. Then for a moment she pauses and says, "Look what I'm going to do for you now!"

From the glove compartment she removes a sex toy, the like of which has never been seen before.

It is a large black rubber ball mounted with threatening luminescent metal spikes. It is impossible even to imagine to what use this object could be put.

"Just watch this, my dear."

And she makes the spiked ball slowly disappear beneath her body, but at that moment . . .

"Jesus Christ!" Julian shouts.

42

A female cry interrupts the music and everything else.

Fred Ballinger switches on the light on the bedside table, looking worried.

Lena wakes with a start covered in sweat. She is struggling for air, still in the grip of a nightmare.

"Lena, what's come over you?"

She is breathing hard, slowly coming back to reality and regaining her normal breathing. She reassures her father: "It's nothing. Nothing. I was having a dream."

"More like a nightmare?"

"Let's say something between the two. It's over now."

Fred switches off the light. In the darkness, Lena turns over to sleep, but remains awake. Their backs are turned to one another.

After some time, she asks a question. "As a man, what do you think of Miss Universe?"

"Complete disappointment."

Lena is cheered by her father's statement. After a pause she adds, "Pa, I have to tell you something . . . something personal."

"What's that, Lena?"

"Julian's a prick, because I'm very good in bed."

"I know."

"What? You know . . . ?"

"You're my daughter. And I myself, modestly speaking, was a little marvel between the sheets."

Gradually, each one in their own corner of the bed, father and daughter put their embarrassment to one side and burst into sniggers in the dark.

43

Fred wanders around a shop filled with souvenirs and bits of local artisan woodwork, shooting the odd disinterested glance at the shelves.

Jimmy Tree goes up to an assistant behind the counter and places a briarwood walking stick on it, proud of having found one similar to the South American's. The assistant starts to gift-wrap it.

While Jimmy is waiting, the pale thirteen-year-old girl from the hotel appears at his side. She is pink around the eyes, which makes her look more upset than disturbing.

She bites her nails nervously while staring at the actor, who notices her and turns around. She studies him quite openly in a manner forthright enough – and for long enough – to make Jimmy feel a little uncomfortable. Then, sure of herself, she starts to speak. "I've seen you in a film."

"You liked 'Mr Q', did you? Everyone does."

"No, I saw you in a film where you play a young father who's never met his son and comes upon him for the first time in a motorway services when the boy's already fourteen."

Jimmy feels like he has turned to stone. He mutters, "No-one's ever seen that film."

"I liked the conversation when your son says, 'Why didn't you want to be a father?' and you say, 'I didn't think I was up to it.' It was then I understood something very important."

"What was that?"

"No-one in the world thinks they're up to it. And so there's no need to worry. See you back at the hotel. *Ciao.*" The girl saunters off as naturally as she came.

Jimmy stands frozen by the counter.

Instinctively, he puts on his sunglasses.

Fred is standing still behind him among the shelves. He must have heard everything, because he finds himself staring at Jimmy's back. Feeling uncomfortable as Jimmy, he says nothing and merely focuses on the actor's shoulders.

44

Jimmy and Fred are walking along a beautiful path through the Alpine countryside.

They are silent, wrapped up in the sounds of cicadas and distant cowbells.

"What do you do all day, Fred?"

"I don't do a thing, so they say I'm apathetic."

"Don't you miss working?"

"Not at all. I've worked too much."

"So what do you miss, then?"

"My wife. I miss my wife, Melanie."

"I read on Wikipedia that you hung around with Stravinsky when you were a young man."

"True."

"What was he like, Stravinsky?"

"He was a very quiet man."

"Quiet? Is that all? Come on, give me a bit more, Fred. I need friends who can give me something. Tell me something about him."

"He once said that intellectuals have no taste. From that

day forward I've done everything I can not to be an intellectual. And I think I've succeeded."

Jimmy says nothing. They continue to walk in silence.

"And you? What do you miss?"

"Fortunately, nothing."

"Come on, Jimmy, give me something more."

Jimmy smiles, as if caught in flagrante. "I discovered what I miss four months ago reading Novalis."

Fred looks surprised. "You've read Novalis?"

"Apart from getting drunk, snorting coke and dating anorexic models, actors in California also sometimes read Novalis," Jimmy replies in jest.

"You're right, I'm sorry. I'm an old man full of prejudices. And what did Novalis say?"

"'I am always going home, always to my father's house.'"

45

Mark Kozelek presses PLAY on an iPod linked up to a pair of speakers and the soft notes of a synthesiser fill the room. The piece is slow and hypnotic. Kozelek's friends concentrate and listen closely to the music. Outside on the terrace of the suite, Jimmy Tree is lying on a sunbed. He is also listening to the piece. He is smoking a cigarette, which he then extinguishes in a cup of tisane. Mark Kozelek comes out and lies down on a sunbed next to him.

"Do you like the piece? I composed it yesterday. It's called 'Ceiling Gazing'."

Jimmy's reply is sincere. "It's wonderful, Mark."

Mark's singing is added to the synthesiser. A romantic voice that sends tingles down the spine.

46

In her room the petite and shy masseuse is gently dancing around. She is playing the Xbox game, but has changed the steps of the dance.

47

The South American is on the balcony in his briefs, half lying on the sun lounger. At his feet, his wife is massaging his huge, painful legs.

His gaze is lost over the valley. All of a sudden, he experiences a vision. Huge floodlights switch on, like those in a football stadium, and he sees twenty-two men split into two formations. One line of eleven wears the Argentinian strip, the other the England strip.

The twenty-two walk up the steep grassy slope and come to the hotel garden.

They form into a single line and wave to a non-existent crowd.

It looks like the moment before the start of an important football match.

The South American stares at this vision, transfixed. His wife lifts her sad gaze and looks at him. She asks him in Spanish, "What are you thinking about?"

The stadium floodlights go out in a single stroke.

"The future," he says.

48

Lena is asleep in the suite's double bed. The room is dark.

Fred is in the little lounge, sitting in the middle of the couch. From here he can see Lena asleep in the bedroom. Then he turns away from her and stares into space. He starts to reflect on things, while his thumb and forefinger rub a sweet wrapper imperceptibly at irregular intervals to produce a simple but beautiful melody.

It is that tiny sound that wakes Lena. She opens one eye. Without getting up, she studies her father sitting in the lounge.

49

The lights are dimmed for the night. At reception, two night porters are hurrying through the formalities for a group of six that has just arrived. They are quite ordinary in appearance, four women and two men, all in their forties. But their luggage consists of strange rigid metal cases.

Then two more women come in carrying metal clothes racks from which hang dozens of costumes protected by suit carriers.

They all seem exhausted.

50

In one part of the hotel is an imitation underground grotto with papier-mâché walls that simulate Alpine rocks.

A long spiral staircase descends below ground and ends directly in a large circular pool that contains dark water and so many mineral salts you can float spread-eagled on your back without any effort.

In fact, in a chosen dark corner, Mick Boyle and his five scriptwriters are floating naked and supine, spread out in haphazard fashion.

They are working out the final scene of "Last Day in a Life".

The scriptwriter with the joking manner makes a suggestion. "He's on the bed, about to die, and whispers to his wife, 'I should have focused on you and our relationship instead of spending my life trying to become an insurance kingpin.'"

"Or he says something ordinary and simple like 'Look after yourself'," adds the scriptwriter who is in love with the girl.

"No, we have to stay with the physical pain right to the end," the intellectual of the group interjects. "He should say, 'Even the morphine doesn't do a thing for me anymore.'"

"And what if his last words are on some insignificant detail? If he says, 'I wonder what became of that horseshoe key ring you gave me twenty-five years ago!'" the girl suggests.

Mick interrupts them. "No. On the point of death on his bed, the man says nothing."

The scriptwriters are silent. They wait.

"It's his wife who speaks. Brenda. And she says, 'Michael, I've lost so much time with you. The best years of my life. I've lost them.'"

Silence. Then the shy scriptwriter says, "And then as he's about to die on the bed, she instinctively gives him a slap."

Mick and the others give him a frosty reception. The shy scriptwriter picks up on it and backtracks. "Only kidding," he says.

51

Mark Kozelek's electronic music spreads softly along the quiet corridor. The group of six people is struggling down it, carrying the metal frames and awkward metallic cases.

Without noticing, the group passes the half-open door of one of the rooms.

Sitting on the bed, naked to the waist, an exhausted old man is covered in sweat. He is looking at the floor and sipping from a glass of water. The chubby homely looking escort girl is standing, slipping on her coat. She leaves and makes for the lift in her graceless, ungainly manner.

52

Again, Kozelek's music is playing.

It is night time in the hotel lobby and a man is gently combing back Jimmy Tree's hair, while Jimmy studies himself in a mirror. It is one of those theatre dressing-room mirrors with lights all around it. The barber then shaves the hair on the back of Jimmy's neck with an electric razor. He cuts it very short. In a taut atmosphere full of suspense, the other people in the lobby are observing the barber at work.

Then, with a neat, expert gesture, he combs Jimmy's fringe to the right. To finish, he dips his hands into a tub of brilliantine.

A middle-aged woman delicately unzips a suit carrier and for an instant a green costume can be seen.

53

The underwater lights in the blue swimming pool give off a magical glow.

With his hair shaved very close on the back of his head, Jimmy Tree is doing a few slow lengths of breaststroke. He then gets out with the short, tired steps of an old man. He dries himself and then dresses, slipping on the trousers of a green military uniform. His face is hidden from us.

In the distance, behind the Alpine peaks, dawn is beginning to break.

54

In military uniform, Adolf Hitler is trying to strut down the long covered walkway in the garden. He succeeds only in part thanks to the help of a briarwood walking stick as he takes short, uncertain steps. This Hitler has aged somewhat, feeling the aches and pains of a man of sixty.

This version of the Führer bears more than a passing resemblance to Jimmy Tree.

Jimmy walks slowly and warily with an austere and dictatorial air, erasing any differences between his character and the real Adolf Hitler. He looks around him, but there is no-one else there.

Then, all of a sudden, this Führer comes to a halt. He places the palm of his hand on his forehead so that he can arrange his hair better, exactly as Mick Boyle often does, and then with a certain emphasis he gives a Nazi salute.

It is directed at Frances, the pale thirteen-year-old, who is now standing in front of him. Jimmy remains with his arm in the air. He is waiting for a reaction. She looks calmly at him and confines herself to smiling at him, not frightened in the least by the performance.

55

Mick Boyle is in a dressing gown in a deckchair beside the beautiful indoor swimming pool.

Lena is swimming gently, effortlessly.

There is no-one there but the two of them.

"I've never told you how very sorry I am about how it's ended up between you and Julian."

Lena stops near the edge of the pool.

"Anyway, I wanted to apologise for his behaviour."

"Apologise? It's not your problem."

"Yeah, but to be honest, I could have done a little more as a father."

"Julian's done what he felt like without worrying about the consequences. He smelled it in the air. I'm starting to smell it myself."

"Smell what?"

Lena smiles. "The heady scent of freedom."

Mick smiles as well. "Yes, I know that smell."

"But, honestly, Pa has never mentioned anything about the Queen, about performing his 'Simple Songs' in London and how he's turned her down?"

"Nothing. Not a word."

"It's a very strange friendship you two have."

"Strange? No, it's a very good friendship. And in good friendships you only talk about the good things. He obviously thought the Queen's invitation wasn't one of them."

"He says that he can't perform 'Simple Songs' because my mother was the only one who could really sing them."

Mick looks surprised. "He said exactly that?"

"Yes, that's what he told the Queen's emissary."

"It's taken him eighty years to say something romantic and who does he say it to? An emissary of the Queen, that's who!"

Lena and Mick smile at each other.

"He watches me at night. And for the first time in my life last night, he gave me a caress while I was sleeping. But I wasn't asleep. Only pretending."

"Yes, parents know when a child is only pretending to sleep."

Lena's eyes are bright with tears and she turns her back on Mick to hide her pain.

"Are you worried about him?"

"No, not at all."

56

We know that this hotel is a very quiet place, but it has never been as quiet as it is now.

Now, that is, that all those present are looking in one direction at a table where – paying them no heed – Adolf Hitler is devoting himself to a hearty breakfast.

The amazing thing is that they are all looking at him with deference, uneasily, as if they have found themselves in front of the real dictator sixty years later, so much so that someone leaving the dining-room ends up giving the Führer a barely perceptible bow and says, "Good morning."

The Führer returns the greeting with a haughty nod.

Then Jimmy's Hitler takes a handkerchief from his pocket, blows into it, rubs it four times across his nose, just as Fred always does, then folds it and puts it back in his pocket.

From his table, Ballinger watches him, and seeing Hitler adopting his own habitual gesture, allows himself a strange smile.

Then the silent German couple stops in front of Jimmy-as-Hitler and the woman glowers at him.

"Never do this again," she orders him.

57

Turned out in mountain-trekking gear – caps, sunglasses, trendy little rucksacks, close-fitting synthetic orange T-shirts, Bermuda hiking shorts, coloured Salomon trekking shoes and walking poles – Fred and Mick are sitting next to each other in a cable car rising up into the blue to a height of three thousand metres. They look up above them, at the sharp summit of a vertiginous rock face, and proceed in silence.

"I spoke to Lena a little this morning. She's worried about you," Mick says after a while.

Fred looks at the peak, no expression on his face. Mick waits, but his friend says nothing.

"It's years since you went to visit Melanie. Why don't you go? Venice is very close."

Fred remains silent. The other man turns to observe him, but Fred only stares at the mountain. Mick tries again. "Lena told me about this business with the Queen. You never told me. You know, it could be a good thing, don't you think? I'd be very happy to hear 'Simple Song, Number 3' one last time in concert."

"I wouldn't."

"You don't want to betray Melanie's memory, but sometimes in order to remain faithful you need to have the courage to betray. Don't you agree?"

After a moment, contemplating the mountain, Fred replies, "Mick, there's one thing that keeps buzzing around in my brain."

"What's that?"

"I wonder what it would have been like to go to bed with Gilda Black!"

Mick is embarrassed. "Yeah, I wonder what it would have been like too!"

Fred turns to study him. He has no faith in Mick's statement. Half serious, half facetious, he whispers, "Liar!"

Mick avoids his gaze.

58

At three thousand metres the silence and the Alps are full of beauty. The only sound at that high altitude is the wind.

Fred and Mick are sitting in an Alpine meadow that slopes down to a far distant valley. There is no-one else around. Only the two of them and nature. And the silence. Fred unwraps a sweet and pops it in his mouth.

After a considerable silence, Fred breaks the gentle soughing of the mountain wind.

"Mick?"

"Eh?"

"Why are we dressed up like this?"

Mick smirks.

In the vast silence, Fred starts to rub the sweet wrapper at musical intervals. The other man looks furtively at his friend's fingers as they play.

"That's not very good!"

"What?"

"The piece you're composing with the sweet wrapper. You've done better in your career."

Now it is Fred's turn to smirk for a moment. Then, with a start, he becomes serious.

In the dark, the escort girl's diminutive mother is holding the hand of her chubby, awkward daughter as they walk along the garden's covered pathway. The fluorescent letters of the word HOTEL stand out above their heads.

They come to the hotel lobby. As usual, the mother gives her daughter a kiss and says to her, "Now do a good job in there."

Her daughter goes in. The mother takes a last look at her.

59

Mick and Fred are sitting on steaming hot wooden benches, wearing skimpy towels to preserve their modesty. They are sweating like pigs and look as if they could expire at any moment.

Not saying a word, exhausted by the monstrous temperature of the sauna, a sudden apparition brings them sharply back to life.

A statuesque woman in a dressing gown has entered the sauna. She takes off her robe.

She is naked underneath.

She is beautiful, perfect, the very definition of sensational. This living creature, for that is what she is, moves with flawless elegance and femininity as she spreads a towel on one of the benches and stretches herself out, oblivious of her own nudity and the two elderly gentlemen present. She closes her eyes and settles down.

Not only is this woman completely at ease, but seemingly born to create unease in others.

Fred and Mick, appropriately ill at ease, stare at her as you would stare at something paranormal – that is, something inexplicable. They take an unreasonable amount of time to make contact with reality again. They start to whisper so as not to be heard by this vision of perfection.

"Who is she?"

"What d'you mean: who is she? It's Miss Universe."

"She looks totally different. Unrecognisable."

"It's that passion for Transformers movies. It's transformed her."

Fred does not laugh. He cannot manage it. He has to look at Miss Universe through the clouds of steam. Her beauty is exhausting.

"You know something, Fred? We talk so much about peeing, we've forgotten that our masculine organs also possess another function."

"Don't delude yourself, Mick."

"Delude myself? Listen, there are certain pills today . . ."

"Yes, but that's pushing at the reality of certain things."

"So? I'm a filmmaker. What else have I done my whole life?"

Miss Universe gently moves her legs a few centimetres, just a little, but delivers yet another blow to her observers.

"But she's not interested, Mick. She's interested in a body that'll match hers. Sex is like music. It wants harmony. And that's only right. And we're not capable of giving harmony anymore, Mick."

They could both have cried at this point, if a member of the staff had not entered and approached them.

"There's a visitor for you, Mr Boyle."

Mick snorts. “Can’t you see we’re enjoying the last great illusion of our lives here? Anyway, who’s the nuisance?”

“Brenda Morel.”

60

Brenda Morel, once that most mysterious of *femmes fatales,* is sitting, impeccably dressed, bolt upright in an armchair. She is well over eighty and has had numerous face-lifts. A small diamond necklace glittering in a light of its own sits comfortably around a wrinkled neck that has endured too much plastic surgery. The mane of blonde hair invites suspicion that it might be a wig.

She is waiting and, as she does so, passes her tongue expertly over her teeth to check if any trace of lipstick is ruining the look of her perfect dentures.

Mick enters the private lounge in a festive mood of joy and affection. But not Brenda. She is serious and reserved.

"Brenda, what a wonderful, beautiful surprise!"

"Hi, Mick."

They kiss each other on the cheeks.

"Brenda, you look incredible. The very picture of radiance."

"You're mistaking me for last century's vintage, Mick."

He laughs exaggeratedly. "So, what's this? You couldn't wait any longer? We've only just finished the latest draft. We were struggling over the last scene and then just yesterday – *boom*! – we nailed it. Now that you're here in person, we can give it to you straightaway. But didn't you say you were staying in L.A.? How come you're here in Europe?"

Brenda looks him seriously in the eye. "How many years have we known each other, Mick?"

"Jesus, that puts me on the spot! Let me count . . ."

"We've known each other for fifty-three years. And how many movies have we made together?"

"Nine, ten . . ."

"Eleven. And do you think that after fifty-three years of friendship and eleven movies I would dish out a bunch of crap to you?"

Mick looks lost. "Well, no, I don't think so . . . I don't think I'd deserve that."

"In fact, you don't deserve it. But what you do deserve is me calling a spade a spade. That's why I've hauled my keyster all the way over here from L.A. to speak with you in person."

Brenda's severe manner gives Mick pause for thought. "O.K. Look, Brenda, if it's about Scene 21 where you're described as 'ugly, falling apart, a shadow of your former beautiful self', you have to realise that it's artistic licence, but naturally on the set we'll proceed in a different manner. I want you to be extraordinary. You still retain that mystery, that fascination that makes you an eternal star."

"Stop kissing my ass, Mick, because you're pissing me off even more, given what I've come here to tell you."

"Why? What have you come here to tell me?"

"I'm pulling out of the film, Mick."

"What?"

"I've been offered a T.V. series in New Mexico. A three-year contract. An alcoholic granny recovering from a bad stroke. A character that pushes her shit to the limit. But I can pay for Jack's rehab, my granddaughter Angelina's film school, the debts of my idiot husband, and I'll even have enough money left over for that villa in Miami that I've been wanting for the last fourteen years. So that's what I've come to tell you."

Mick starts to protest and raises his voice. "But this is cinema, Brenda. The other's just television! And you know television's shit."

"It's the future, Mick. Or rather, to tell you the truth, it's already the present. And let's be clear, because in this freaking world nobody ever speaks clearly. You're in your eighties and, like so many of your colleagues, you get worse the older you get. The last three films you made, Mick, are nothing but crap. But, I'll say this, as do many others: they're not the usual crap!"

Mick Boyle is about to have a heart attack. He has to scream, even though he cannot allow himself to, given his age and high blood pressure. "How dare you! Yeah, how dare you! You want to be clear? O.K., let's be clear. If it wasn't for me – who was, is and always will be a gentleman – you'd still be on your knees under the desks of those producers way back then. Fifty-three years ago I pulled you out of the boxer shorts of those flabby producers and made you a star."

Brenda is incandescent. She also screams at the top of her voice. "You piece of shit! I was fine inside those boxer shorts! And you know why? Because I *wanted* to be there. I don't have to thank anybody. I've done everything myself. I paid for the Actors Studio by cleaning every last john in Brooklyn. My mother went into debt for me. And I walked into Hollywood through the main gate thanks to me and myself alone. Marilyn, Rita and Grace all shit themselves when they saw me coming. It's all there in my autobiography. You read it?"

"Yes, I have, unfortunately. But it wasn't you who wrote it. And it was a crap autobiography, just like it's a crap T.V. series you're now off to do."

Brenda gasps, as if struggling for air, and then surprisingly, she stops shouting. She is calm. She begins to talk quietly and this makes her even more pitiless than when she was screaming. "No, it's your film that's crap, Mick. I know the movies and you know I do. It's you who doesn't get it anymore, because you're old, you're tired, and you don't know how to see the world anymore, because all you can see is your own death, waiting for you just around the corner. Your career's over, Mick. I'm telling you straight because I'm fond of you. No-one's interested in your last will and testament of a film and it risks wiping out all the decent films you made. And that would be inexcusable. It was only going to be made because I was in it. So I'm going to save your life by not being in it. And your dignity."

Mick, exhausted, has no more strength. He manages a barbed whisper. "You're ungrateful. Ungrateful and a moron. And that's how you made your career."

The insults no longer affect Brenda. Or perhaps she simply does not believe them to be true. Instead she stretches out a hand dripping with diamonds and does something outrageous. With Mick on the verge of tears, she caresses his cheek and says, "Yes, Mick, that's true. You're right."

Vengeful and full of venom, Mick hisses, "I'm going to make this film anyway. Even without you."

Now Mick is crying. She continues to brush his cheek. "There, there, Mick, life goes on. Even without the bullshit movies."

But Mick has lost heart, he puts his head in his hands.

And the last of the old Hollywood stars gets to her feet, straightens out the little creases in her dress, grabs hold of her thirty thousand dollar handbag and, with controlled regal poise, walks out of the hotel lounge.

61

The end of spring is approaching. That means this evening sees the performance of the mime artist, with all the trimmings: white tie and tails, face made up to look supremely sad.

The man who was covered in mud approaches Miss Universe.

"Do you know that you're a very beautiful example of a human being?"

"Do you know what, I was just thinking the same thing myself."

The man goes off without another word.

The mime artist is pretending to climb an imaginary wall, without much success.

Jimmy Tree, dressed in his own clothes again, sits close to Mick to watch the show. Fred and Lena are at the table with them.

Mick is in a catatonic state. He watches, but sees nothing. Staring into space, he says in a monotone voice, "You know how many actresses I've worked with in my career?"

"A good many . . . I suppose."

Mick gives vent to his feelings. "More than fifty. I have

launched the careers of at least fifty actresses. And they've all been very grateful. I . . . I am a great director of women."

Fred and Lena turn to look at Mick and neither can find the right words.

Jimmy Tree looks Mick in the eye and recites a line: "'*That way, and only that way, Frank, you'll never forget me.*' Remember that line, Mr Boyle?"

"I remember all the films I've made."

"Mr Boyle, you're not just a great director of women. You're a great director, period."

Exhausted from his failed bid to climb the wall, the mime artist curls up on the floor and pretends to go to sleep.

Fred Ballinger is watching him.

Lena is watching her father.

The mountaineer is staring at Lena.

A brief round of applause greets the mime artist.

The audience starts to disperse. The evening's entertainment is over. Mick, Fred and Lena are preparing to leave as well, when the boy violinist calls out to them, "Mr Ballinger."

The group turns round. The boy has jumped on the stage and, violin in hand, starts playing the first notes of "Simple Song, Number 3". He is only able to play the first two chords, but has improved compared with his earlier attempts. He performs them well; although repetitive, the sweetness of the notes has an effect.

As if time has been suspended, everyone there is hypnotised by the boy's simple execution: Jimmy Tree, Mark Kozelek and his friends, the mountaineer, Lena, the South American and his wife, the German couple, the elderly and their carers, the vulgar Russians, the African-American family, Frances and her mother, the waiters, the doctor, the hotel manager and the chefs. It is just like the end of a crime drama when all the main characters and the extras are gathered together.

But only one of them is really moved by those simple notes on the violin and it is not Fred Ballinger. Mick Boyle's eyes are the ones moist with tears.

And Fred Ballinger is the only one who notices.

Lena is at the foot of the free-climbing wall at an hour when the gym is empty. Still dressed in her elegant evening gown, she is studying the height of the imitation rock wall.

The mountaineer must have followed her there, because he is standing behind her, wary and shy, but desperate to make contact. He is a bundle of nerves and embarrassment. He straightens his shirt, runs a hand through his hair, and then comes to stand by her side. Lena ignores him, as if he does not exist. He attempts a clumsy invitation. "Would you like to try a climb?"

Only at this point does Lena suddenly turn to him. She pierces him with a look that could not be more sensual, and says to him, seriously, darkly, "You know, if I want, I can drive a man crazy in bed?"

As if it were the most natural thing to do, the mountaineer raises his eyes to heaven, turns white as a *mozzarella* and falls with a thud to the ground.

Lena immediately stops acting the *femme fatale* and takes on the role of the concerned friend, cursing to herself, "Oh, hell's bells!"

She leans down close to the mountaineer lying on the floor and starts patting his cheeks in an effort to revive him. She is frightened. "Mr Moroder, Mr Moroder! Wake up, damn you!"

The mountaineer slowly opens his eyes again. He finds Lena's worried face a few centimetres from his own.

In a faint voice he says, "It is not necessary for you to sleep with a man to drive him crazy."

She smiles, reassured.

The homely escort girl is sitting sad and alone on a couch. The lobby is deserted. Mick appears behind her and without further ado says to her, "O.K., I've made up my mind and have some money from the cash machine."

The girl turns and looks at him. "And what would you like to do?"

Mick is serious. "Take a walk."

Down the garden dotted with age-old trees, Mick Boyle and the graceless escort girl walk hand in hand like two sweethearts in the first flush of love.

And that is all they do, walk slowly along without looking at one another, their hands joined, alone.

On the other hand, the two scriptwriters Mick Boyle predicted would fall in love have actually done so. They are kissing each other on a secluded bench with that intensity of first love. Endless and exhausting. Suddenly, out of the corner of her eye, but without stopping her kissing, the young woman glimpses Mick and the young escort walking by.

62

On a bench on the platform of the small local train station, the five scriptwriters and Mick Boyle sit glumly, waiting for a train. The two lovers are hand in hand.

After a silence, Mick breaks the ice. "Come on, kids, what are all these long faces for? Glitches and hang-ups are par for the course in our business. Get used to it. I've already spoken to the producer – we need time to get a new actress and then we start shooting. We'll only have to wait a few more months."

"What a shit, that Brenda Morel," the intellectual scriptwriter says.

"Don't talk about her like that."

"She's just an opportunist," the scriptwriter in love says.

"No different from the rest of us," Mick replies. "And it's what you have to be to survive in this jungle."

"And it's not true she came to Europe just to see you, Mick. I read she's going to Cannes, to some gala benefit."

The team shoot dirty looks at the shy scriptwriter who has just spoken.

"Now let's not go too far with all this reality. Remember illusion is our business."

"Your lasting testimony is worth much more than yet another T.V. series, Mick," the team's clown says.

"My lasting testimony? Let's not exaggerate. Most people die without anyone taking any notice, never mind leaving a lasting testimony."

The intellectual speaks again. "But most people aren't great artists like you."

"It makes no difference. People, artists, animals, plants – we're nothing but extras on the set."

The train comes in, the doors open.

The young scriptwriters grab hold of their rucksacks and get on the train. The woman, who up till now has been silent, gets on last. Mick remains on the platform and looks up. Before the door closes, she turns round to Mick and with a beautiful smile says, "He's on the point of death and he dies. Only then, for the first time, she says to him, 'Michael, I love you.'"

Mick is touched and smiles back. "Perfect!"

The door closes. The train pulls away and disappears round a bend. A downcast Mick turns on his heel and leaves the station.

63

Looking old and disappointed, Mick shuffles along the path through the valley. It is a magnificent day. Bright sunshine in a clear blue sky. The air is crystal clear. The cicadas are in full swing. An Edenic scene.

A female voice, coming from who knows where, calls out to him: "Mick!"

Mick turns to his left towards a huge uncultivated meadow. He looks, but can see no-one. Then out of the long grass pops a woman dressed as a 1950s air hostess. It was she who called his name, and she now adds in an anxious voice, "Mick, how should I say this line? I don't get it."

Mick has no time to reply because another woman has emerged from the grass. She looks like a young Jean Seberg, wearing a bikini. She speaks as if she were delivering a line of dialogue in a film in the arch tones of a snob. "James, perhaps you don't realise I never set foot on a yacht less than twenty-five metres long."

Then from out of the grass springs a ditzy early 1960s blonde with a great cleavage, also delivering a line of dialogue:

"Oh, that's enough! Come on now, boys, where have you hidden my little purple slippers?"

Mick looks at her and gives a radiant smile.

A woman in her fifties then pops up dressed as a lay nun and acts her part, on the verge of tears. "Albert, you don't know what it has cost me to preserve my virginity until today! Until you!"

A magnificent countess in nineteenth-century costume then delivers one of her lines to her prince: "Sire, I possess six castles and twenty carriages, but I can state only one thing with certainty: life is very tedious."

Lastly there is a woman dressed as a 1968 left-wing militant. "Sure, we all want a revolution, so long as we don't have to work too hard at it."

Mick looks happily at each of his actresses. One by one, they all recite lines from his films.

A woman of thirty-five springs up from the grass. With a flowing mane of red hair, her shoulders bare, she looks wonderful, oozing fascination, and she says in a sensual voice full of nostalgia, "Alright then, I will sleep with you, but on one condition: you are not to have an orgasm. That way, and only that way, Frank, you'll never forget me."

All of Mick's actresses line up like skittles, one behind the other, each delivering one of her lines. Those who appeared first continue to repeat the same line at a lower volume.

In short, a crucible of actresses is created, each one superimposed on top of the other, in all shapes and ages and different types of costume (a female soldier, a little old grandmother, a drag king, a sultry vamp, a singer, a gymnast, a ballerina in a tutu, and many others), all spread about the field.

Again the air hostess complains, "How do you want her, Mick? Honest and sincere or vain, fatuous and evil? And how should I walk? How does this character move?"

Mick is about to reply when yet another actress rising up from the grass catches his attention. And this is the one, more than all the others, that chokes Mick up, and he calls out instinctively, "Mother!"

All the other actresses fall silent now, handing the stage to this late arrival.

It is Brenda Morel dressed in a cheap dressing gown, ugly, decrepit, a fading shadow of her former beauty, who says in neutral tones, "My son, you were so handsome as a boy. And the really obscene thing is that you've remained a handsome man. Handsome and useless."

Mick's eyes are bright with tears in the silence of the empty meadow. He is alone. The daydream is over.

64

Fred and Mick are in Fred's bedroom.

One is sitting in an armchair; the other is on the edge of the bed, looking out of the window. Calm and resigned, Fred eyes his friend, knowing what a difficult time he is going through.

"Have you spoken to the producer?"

Mick turns to observe him, "Fred, I've been in the business long enough to know that if Brenda refuses to be in it, this movie will never get made."

Silence. Mick reflects a moment. His eyes come to rest on Fred's bedside table. He studies the photograph of Fred hugging his wife ten years earlier. Old but happy, and still good-looking.

"Melanie looks so beautiful in that photo."

"Yes, that's true. She does look beautiful."

"You know, Fred, there's one thing I've learned. People can be either good-looking or they can be ugly. In the middle are the nice ones."

Fred gives a bitter smile, which Mick returns with interest.

“This vacation’s coming to an end. What are you going to do next, Fred?”

“What do you think I’m going to do? Go home. Get back into the old routine.”

“Not me. I don’t know how to live a routine life. You know what I’m going to do, Fred? I’m going to dedicate myself to another film. You said emotions were overrated, but that’s bullshit. Emotions are all we have.”

Mick gets up, goes over to the window, opens it and steps out onto the balcony. And with exaggerated nonchalance he puts one foot on the wicker chair, the other on the windowsill, and lets himself drop from the fourth floor.

Fred had time to get to his feet, but Mick was too quick and unpredictable to give him any chance to save him.

65

The Boeing aircraft is stationary on the runway. In the background stand the Alps.

The aircraft is full; the passengers sit without moving.

A hostess walks along the aisle. She politely addresses a distinguished-looking gentleman. "I'm sorry, sir, you have to switch the mobile off."

Suddenly, from the other half of the plane, from business class, separated by a curtain, a monstrous raucous shrieking is heard. It continues, a dynamic sound that is intermittent yet piercing.

Everyone strains their neck in surprise towards business class.

The hostess runs as fast as she can in that direction.

The cries continue – a female voice, and one in great distress, it would seem. More female cries ensue, along with the sounds of a scuffle.

The shouting now grows faint.

The passengers are on their feet and looking ahead of them. From up near the pilot's cabin and the forward exit, we can hear only the sound of voices talking over one another, a muffled cry of pain, a confused disturbance.

At the centre of the disturbance, five hostesses, overwrought by the exertion, are struggling to immobilise a person stretched out on the floor. One of them is bleeding from a cut on her lip.

The person they are restraining is moaning, writhing, as if in extremis.

It is Brenda Morel, stretched out on the floor in a terrible state. Her dress is torn, revealing an old woman's flesh-coloured petticoat, her make up has gone awry, her face is unrecognisable, distorted by pain and tears as she utters incomprehensible unfinished words that are more than a little disturbing.

She is also bald. Her wig must have been lost in the scuffle with the cabin crew.

Now we can understand what she is saying. She mutters in exhaustion, but determinedly, to the hostesses holding her down, "You shitty bitches, let me get off this asshole of a plane immediately!"

The pilot emerges from his cabin, visibly out of breath. He address Brenda: "Alright, Miss Morel, you win. I have authorisation from the control tower. We can now let you off the plane."

66

The usual cows are spread about a meadow with their bells chiming at random.

Fred is sitting on a rock facing them. He watches them without stirring.

Then he closes his eyes.

He raises his arm as if to direct an orchestra, but this time nothing happens.

The bells continue to ring out in anarchic fashion.

With his eyes closed, Fred performs a gesture of anxious frustration. He then moves his arm again, with more energy, but still nothing. He cannot manage to shut himself off and compose.

He needs music, but music still has no need of him. He opens his eyes, the cows are still there in front of him. He shouts a ridiculous order at them: "Be quiet."

But the cows and their bells ignore him.

Fred lets his head fall a little. He is exhausted. His eyes are bright with pain.

A surprising thing then happens. Without any warning

sign, a paraglider silently lands among the cows.

Fred watches him. The paragliding wings fall and land on the man, covering him. The man laboriously frees himself, then looks around in surprise, realising that he has arrived in the wrong place.

He walks up to Fred and calmly says to him, "I don't think I should have landed here."

And without waiting for any response, he marches off along the hillside.

Fred follows him with his gaze and, despite his tears, he smiles.

67

A stupendous bow window looking out onto the Alps. It houses an ancient wooden birdcage. A beautiful circular object that is home to a magnificent blackbird.

The bird is singing a simple song that borders on perfection.

This is the office of the sixty-year-old doctor. He is on his feet, looking distressed and dismayed, staring at Fred Ballinger, who is sitting on the other side of the desk, in raptures at the blackbird's song.

The doctor is saying tactfully, "You'll be going to Los Angeles for the funer—"

Fred cuts him off: "Sssshhhhhh!"

The doctor falls silent.

Glassy-eyed, Fred gets to his feet and goes over to the bow window to listen to the blackbird up close.

The doctor also turns to observe the bird, which, for no reason, suddenly stops singing.

Fred turns to the doctor and says in a single breath, "What wonderful artists birds are! No, I'm not going to Los Angeles.

I'm not going to Mick Boyle's funeral. And I won't be coming here for my holidays again. It's perfectly pointless coming back to the places where one has been happy. One has to learn to face the rest of life."

The doctor nods gloomily.

"Why have you asked me into your office, doctor? What did you want to say to me?"

The doctor sits on his desk. He picks up a clinical file and opens it. "I have the results of all the check-ups you've had these past weeks."

"What do they say?"

"You're as sound as a bell, Mr Ballinger."

Almost hoping for the worst, Fred says, "But the prostate?"

The other man looks surprised. "Your prostate? You've never had any prostate problems. And if you've never had any so far, you certainly won't have any now."

Fred raises his eyes to look at the doctor. In a most unexpected manner, he smiles and says, "So I'm old, but we don't know why I'm old."

The doctor gives him a smile tinged with sadness.

Through the window Fred can make out the distant figure of the young masseuse walking quickly through the garden in her uniform. The young girl's movements are rapid and smooth. And as Fred follows her with his usual melancholy gaze the doctor says, "And so, do you know what's waiting for you after this?"

"No, doctor, what's that?"

"Youth." He smiles, a sad, reflective smile. "Mick Boyle often dropped in here for a chat."

Fred sees the masseuse disappear behind the line of trees into the indoor swimming pool and then asks the doctor, "Did he ever mention a Gilda Black, by any chance?"

"He spoke of nothing else."

Fred rouses himself, overcome with curiosity. But he hides it so he can hear what he wants to hear.

"Was she his girlfriend?"

"'Girlfriend' would be going too far, I think. All that happened between them is that once, as teenagers, they walked around together in a park holding hands."

Fred grins to himself.

"He called it 'the moment I learned to ride a bicycle'. He never spoke to you about it?"

"No. We only ever talked about the good things."

68

Venice is a beautiful place. And how! So full of mystery. So unique.

At night, however, it seems desolate, deserted. Even the most dedicated tourists have fallen into the arms of Morpheus.

Canals, *calli*, Piazza San Marco. Motionless as statues.

Then a figure appears in the distance, small and vulnerable, the shuffling footsteps of an old man. He holds flowers in his hand. It is Fred Ballinger making his solitary way through the city. He crosses a small bridge. Below him a motor launch passes by in near silence.

A water taxi creates ripples against the side of the cemetery. Fred is sitting on board, looking sad and weary, gazing into space, holding the flowers in his lap.

It is dawn and he is walking along the long gravel pathways dotted with tombs. He is looking for one in particular. He peers at certain names, but cannot remember. His sense of direction was never great.

Then, at last, he finds it. Facing him now is the tomb of Igor Stravinsky. But the flowers remain firmly in his hands.

Fred now knows the way. He walks along a narrow alley beside a canal. He turns and stops. He looks up and sees the plaque of a private clinic.

69

Fred is standing in the sober but expensively furnished private single room of the clinic, holding the flowers in his hand. He is looking at something. He sees a bed next to a window and, facing away from him, an elderly woman with unkempt hair is resting her forehead against the pane.

Fred places the flowers in a small plastic vase on the bedside table. Then he takes the photograph he had in the hotel from his pocket and puts it beside the flowers. He sits down by the woman, who remains with her back to him.

He looks at the floor, overcome by an unfamiliar shyness, and says, "I waited until visiting hours to come and see you."

He then stares at the woman's back under the sheet.

There is no expression on Fred's face.

There is no sound at all.

Then, in a flat voice without any emotion, he starts to speak slowly and simply.

"They have no idea, Melanie. Children have no idea. They can't imagine what their parents are about. Yes, they know certain aspects, the exceptional things . . . those they know. And they know enough to takes sides against each other. They feel a need to simplify matters. And they're right. But they don't know. They can't know. They don't know how I trembled the first time I saw you on stage. And the orchestra, which had understood, was laughing behind my back about my falling in love, my unexpected fragility. They don't know that you sold your mother's jewels to allow me to finish my second work, when everyone was turning me down and saying I was an awkward and presumptuous composer. They don't know that you too at the time – and you were right – thought I was an awkward and presumptuous composer, while you were crying day and night not because you'd sold some jewels, but because you felt you'd sold your mother. They don't know how much you loved me and I loved you. Only we know. They don't know what, despite everything, we've meant to each other. That 'despite everything' that has been so wearing, painful and evil. Melanie, they can never understand that we liked to think of ourselves, despite it all, as a simple song."

He has finished. He gets up from the chair, stands on tiptoe as if to see his wife's face, but gives up straightaway. Emotionally, he is not capable. So he contents himself with stretching out a hand and moving her arm a few centimetres to settle her in a position he thinks will be more comfortable.

70

Fred leaves the hospital. Behind him, on the mezzanine floor, his wife can be seen with her resting forehead against the glass, mouth open.

But from where he is she seems far away.

Fred has stopped, lost in thought. He is about to turn round and look up at his wife's face, but cannot do it. He gives up the attempt and stares once more into the distance. He then takes a sweet from his pocket, unwraps it and slips it into his mouth.

He tries again to turn and look at his wife, who is still there, far away behind the pane of glass, looking out but seeing nothing. Once again, Fred cannot find the strength to look up at his wife's face.

He has the sweet wrapper in his fingers, but does not stroke it; instead he contents himself with throwing it in the canal in front of him.

Vacant, worn out and pushed to his limit, Fred pauses to reflect once more. And the solo violin from "Simple Song, Number 3" starts up in his head and this time it is a great violinist playing it, not a young beginner.

71

Two gilded seats stand empty in expectant silence.

An elegant audience fills the theatre.

Without a prompt or announcement, the audience rises to its feet in ghostly silence. Two figures have entered the theatre: Queen Elizabeth II and Prince Philip.

They sit down in the elegant seats, their royal persons caught in the shadow cast by the stage lights.

The audience can now be seated.

A violinist once more takes up the first soft notes of the introduction to "Simple Song, Number 3. Adagio".

In the shadows, Prince Philip's eyes are full of joy, like a child's.

On stage, the great South Korean soprano Sumi Jo secretly swallows, hiding her anxiety and emotion. She is preparing herself.

Also in the shadows, Queen Elizabeth looks at her husband a moment and is content.

Hiding away in a box, still a bag of nerves, the emissary is watching the Queen and Prince Philip from a distance.

Sumi Jo opens her mouth and when she launches into a perfect, heart-rending love song it seems to reach right to the back of the auditorium.

The members of the large, supremely elegant audience give a slight start in their seats, as if hypnotised by the soprano's voice.

Sumi Jo's high note ends. It lasted only a short while.

Totally focused, in absolute control of himself, Fred Ballinger makes a sweeping gesture with his baton and the whole orchestra comes into play. Strings and woodwind open in unison with a soaring melody, and the audience comes out in goose pimples.

Sitting in the audience on his own, with no friends around him, Jimmy Tree sits slowly forward in his seat; his eyes are bright with childlike fervour.

"Simple Song, Number 3" is beautiful and heart-wrenching.

72

The faces of Lena and the hippy mountaineer are almost touching.

They could kiss each other if it were not for the fact that she is trembling.

He laughs like an idiot. They are so close. Then he stops laughing.

He looks at her. He clasps her powerfully. She stops trembling and looks at him.

We know they will kiss, but not just yet.

Lena and the mountaineer are suspended in mid-air at a height of four thousand metres, nothing but empty space below them. She has her arms around him and the two are clinging on to life thanks to a rope and a set of karabiners.

73

A movement of Fred's arm and the strings and woodwind grow faint and fall silent. Only a solo violin remains.

Fred turns to look at Sumi Jo. With a flicker of his eyes, he gives her the cue.

Sumi Jo breaks out into song again, another clamorous and drawn-out high-pitched note.

Fred can only stare at the South Korean soprano as she reaches that high note. She stares back at him.

Fred continues to observe her, but it is as if he is looking at another person . . .

74

His wife, Melanie.

On the mezzanine floor of the hospital.

Her white hair dishevelled, her face ravaged by illness, eyes distant and mouth open, as if she were singing.

75

Open-mouthed, Sumi Jo is still in the middle of a high note.

Fred Ballinger looks at her, perfectly able to disguise his feelings.

Sumi Jo meets his eyes. She waits. And on a crisp movement of Fred's hand, she suddenly and skilfully brings that exceptional note to an end.

The orchestra moves on to the coda.

And with a sharp and definitive sweep of the baton, Fred Ballinger signals an end to the music.

The orchestra plays no more.

Total silence. The world has stopped turning.

The queen's emissary breathes a huge sigh of relief.

It is over.

Jimmy Tree is bolt upright in his chair, his mouth half open, caught between amazement and emotion. He waits to see what will happen next.

With masterly control, Fred Ballinger slowly turns to face the audience. He shows no satisfaction, not at this moment.

He is impassive, a sphinx, a professional. That is what he is: a consummate professional.

The audience stare up at him from below, all eyes glistening.

Fred Ballinger waits for them to master their emotions. He knows it will take a few seconds before the applause begins.

Of course they will applaud, but not at this moment. Not just yet.

Paolo Sorrentino
April 2014

PAOLO SORRENTINO is an Italian director, scriptwriter and novelist. His film "La Grande Bellezza" was the winner of an Academy Award and a Golden Globe for Best Foreign Language Film and a BAFTA for Best Film not in English. His first novel *Hanno tutti ragione* (Everybody's Right) was shortlisted for Italy's Premio Strega, its most highly regarded literary prize.

N. S. THOMPSON is a poet and a translator from the Italian. His translations include three acclaimed crime novels by Roberto Costantini and *Sicilian Uncles*, a collection of novellas by Leonardo Sciascia.